Three Voices

Three Voices

An Invitation to Poetry
Across the Curriculum

Bernice E. Cullinan

Marilyn C. Scala

Virginia C. Schroder

with

Ann K. Lovett

Stenhouse Publishers
York, Maine

Stenhouse Publishers, 226 York Street, York, Maine 03909

Credits are on page 135.

Library of Congress Cataloging-in-Publication Data
Cullinan, Bernice E.
    Three voices : an invitation to poetry across the curriculum /
Bernice E. Cullinan, Marilyn C. Scala, Virginia C. Schroder with Ann
K. Lovett.
       p.   cm.
    Includes bibliographical references.
    ISBN 1-57110-015-6 (alk. paper)
    1. Poetry—Study and teaching (Elementary)   2. Interdisciplinary
approach in education.   3. Language experience approach in
education.   I. Scala, Marilyn C., 1942–   . II. Schroder, Virginia
C., 1939– . III. Title.
LB1575.C86   1995
372.64—dc20   95-2686
                                     CIP

Cover and interior design by Catherine Hawkes
Cover illustration by Anne Hunter
Typeset by Compset Inc.

Manufactured in the United States of America on acid-free paper

04 03 02 01 00   8 7 6 5 4 3

In memory of the poetry and love

Alfred Holt Colquitt,

Jonathan Cullinan,

Lois Lovett Drewes,

Kelly Miscall

brought into our lives

"To live in hearts we leave behind is not to die."
—Thomas Campbell

Our team worked on poetry, a topic close to our hearts, and shared difficult times when tragedy marked our lives. At first we thought it a coincidence that we formed a circle of love to mourn the loss of beloved children. We came to recognize that our mission to spread the joy of poetry among children is more than coincidental. Our work, like a pebble tossed into water, is part of an ever-widening circle.

Contents

PART ONE
Developing a Love of Poetry

PART TWO
Discovering How Poetry Works

PART THREE
Using Poetry in Content Areas

Preface

Bernice E. Cullinan

I am a teacher who has taught with poetry most of my life; recently I also became a poetry editor. Now, in addition to using poetry with children and encouraging other teachers to do the same, I search for poets and urge them to develop new poetry collections. All of the work I do centers on the magical moment when children fall in love with words: they notice that the sounds of language fall gently on the ear, they discover double meanings, and they notice the playfulness of language. When that happens, children discover poetry and, most often in this process, a teacher, a parent, or a librarian is involved. In my work, I meet teachers who exhibit great enthusiasm for poetry; they use it naturally and frequently in their classrooms and they are filled with ideas about poetry. I find ways, such as this book, to tell others about those ideas.

When I question teachers about how I can help them use poetry in the classroom, they say, "Don't ask us to add one more thing to the curriculum! We're already over-scheduled and we're dancing as fast as we can. Help us find ways to use poetry to do what we need to do anyway. Take what we already do and wrap poetry around it."

The teachers whom I've questioned propose integrating poetry across the curriculum—an idea consistent with literature-based programs, and an approach I applaud. They suggest using poetry to teach social studies, science, math, reading, writing, oral language, drama, and listening skills. This book is an effort to help you do that; it is written *by* teachers *for* teachers, to make your job a little easier and a lot more fun.

Students develop a love of poetry when teachers use it wisely as a natural part of every day. An observer who sees a classroom filled with

What Poems Do:

- tell stories
- make us laugh
- make us cry
- develop a sense of wonder
- show us beautiful language
- create images
- help us see the world in a new way

children who love poetry may think that this happened by chance or that this is just an unusual group. More careful inspection reveals, however, that a teacher knowingly creates a social and physical environment in which a love of poetry grows. This may be as simple as piling many poetry books around the classroom, grabbing a poem that captures a special feeling or moment, or sharing spontaneously a memorized verse. More likely, the students' positive attitude toward poetry results from a plan that includes thematic poetry units, poetry in all curriculum areas, students writing poems, and other activities that call attention to poetry. As teachers, we can experience the joy of giving poetry to another generation of children, expanding their language and enriching their lives. We benefit, too, because we cannot give beauty to children without the scent of roses clinging to our hands.

Teachers Build a Love of Poetry by:

. . . .

- enabling students to make connections with poetry
- surrounding children with poems related to topics of study
- letting children find their favorite poems
- finding poems students like and reading them aloud
- encouraging students to read poems aloud
- helping students build anthologies of favorite poems
- encouraging students to keep poetry journals
- infecting children with a contagious enthusiasm for poetry

Poetry is meant to be read aloud; do it every day. A love of poetry is more caught than taught.

Plan of Organization

You will hear three voices in this book: my voice as the narrator and the voices of two elementary school teachers. I am a professor at New York University who teaches teachers, is active in professional organizations, and travels around the world meeting with teachers. I look for outstanding teachers wherever I go; when I learn about an exciting idea from one teacher, I pass it on to others. My editor, Ann Lovett, who helped us develop this manuscript, introduced me to two outstanding teachers, Virginia (Ginnie) Schroder and Marilyn Scala from Munsey Park School, Manhasset, N.Y. When I saw what Marilyn and Ginnie do with poetry, I wanted others to know about their work. We developed a format for this book in which they speak directly to readers in the vignettes to describe what happens in their classrooms. Ginnie Schroder currently teaches sixth grade but has also taught nursery school, first, third, and fifth grades. Ginnie will describe daily classroom routines as she integrates poetry with all subjects. Marilyn Scala is currently a special education teacher but has also taught first and second grades. Marilyn works with students across all elementary-school levels and leads poetry workshops for children and their teachers.

In each section that follows you will find:

- a description of a strategy that is applicable to many situations

- a vignette by Marilyn or Ginnie telling how the strategy worked in their classrooms

- a list of extensions—ways the strategy can be adapted to other situations

- examples of student work as they applied the strategies.

There is a general developmental progression throughout the book, but there is no particular sequential order to the strategies. You can use any strategy in any order that appeals to you. When the school assembly is postponed at the last moment, or when the art teacher must cancel class due to an emergency, this book should give you a creative idea to put into use immediately. We hope that if you use the flip test on this book, several ideas will stand out for you to give you a choice.

We organized the book into three sections: developing a love of poetry, helping students discover how poetry works, and using poetry in the content areas. Although you can choose from any section, we believe that developing a love of poetry comes before calling attention to specific poetic details or using poetry to underscore content-area learning.

Why Poetry?

Poems are tiny, well-crafted pieces of word work; they contain multiple layers of meaning. Their words reflect subtle shadows, images, and symbols that lead children to see beyond the literal and surface-level meanings. Poetry urges all of us to use higher-level thinking skills because it always suggests there's more than meets the eye—there are subtle meanings if we will seek them out. Poetry leads us to create mental images; it teaches us to imagine, which is basic to language and intellectual growth. Poetry helps us to envision a world we cannot see but one that we can visualize in our mind's eye. It helps us to imagine a world we would like to live in that is better than the one we *do* live in. If we cannot dream of a better world, it is unlikely we can ever create one. Poetry nourishes the imagination.

Reading, writing, listening, and speaking are totally interconnected; they are all part of language and are learned under exactly the same conditions. What we learn in one language area helps us to learn in other areas, because the human mind makes connections between what we already know and what we are trying to learn. For example, if we learn to read new words, we call upon them when we write. If we hear new words in poetry, they become part of a vocabulary we understand. We then draw upon them when we speak, write, and read. Poetry is especially appropriate for language learning (see "Poetry in the Classroom" sidebar), because it contains language used in its most beautiful forms. It fills our language storehouse with interesting words. Children wrap it easily around their tongues and play with its sounds.

Conditions for Learning

Cambourne (1987) studied the conditions we provide for children's language learning and literacy development. He found that the conditions under which children learn to talk are:

Immersion: surround them with language

Demonstration: give them models or demonstrations

Expectation: send subtle messages that we expect them to succeed

Responsibility: let them take charge of what they learn

Approximation: accept attempts, praise them for being close

Employment: give them time to practice what they learn

Feedback: respond to content, not the form, of what they say

Poetry is a shorthand for beauty; its words can cause us to tremble, to shout for joy, to weep, to dance, to shudder, or to laugh out loud. Robert Frost said, "Poetry begins in delight and ends in wisdom."

Poetry speaks to children in ways we cannot fully understand. Perhaps its comforting rhythms and steady beat echo the sound of a mother's heartbeat as it soothes a child still in the womb. Perhaps its melodies and its sounds recall lullabies sung to a child in infancy. Whatever its appeal—it exceeds our comprehension.

Children turn gratefully to poetry for its cathartic and healing effects. Poetry touches the soul in ways we do not understand. During the Nazi Holocaust, children in the Theresienstadt Concentration Camp wrote poems to relieve the horror of their lives and to give voice to their heartache. Their tragic poems appear in *I Never Saw Another Butterfly* (Children in the Theresienstadt Concentration Camp [1964] 1993). Poetry is therapeutic—it allows us to express our deepest emotions and to share the deep feelings others express in their poems.

The language of poems can make us laugh, wonder, or gasp with recognition. Poetry gives substance to abstract concepts, such as creating a community, explorations, pioneers, freedom, honor, or integrity. Concepts and images become clear through the vivid words of poetry.

Poetry in the Classroom
. . . .
Poetry supports language learning because it:
- contains highly charged words
- uses only a few words to say a great deal
- is melodic; it sings as it says
- contains rhythm, repetition, and rhyme
- captures the essence of a concept
- says more than it says/has layers of meaning
- is the natural language of childhood

Poetry Promotes Literacy

All children need poetry. Primarily, poetry helps children to *learn language,* to learn *about* language, and to learn *through* language in the following ways.

Poetry Helps Children Learn to Listen

Children pay attention to poetry because it plays with the sounds of language and uses interesting words that intrigue them. Subtle sound variations delight the mind and lead to new meanings for ears attuned to language. The subtleties, sound patterns, and rhymes rivet the attention to draw listeners closer.

Poetry Helps Increase Children's Vocabulary

Children learn to talk when they are surrounded with talk and are expected to communicate with others. They use the language they hear; if they hear ordinary language, they use ordinary language when they speak. If they hear poetic language, they use poetic language when they speak.

Poetry Helps Children Learn to Read

Beginning readers can learn to decode print in poems because the lines are short, the words rhyme, and the accent falls on meaningful words. These clues tell readers what should be coming next in the text. When children read or hear: "There was an old woman who lived in a shoe/She had so many children she didn't know what to _____/" they can predict that the next word will rhyme with shoe—it must be *do*. We call this kind of language "predictable" because the natural rhythm, repetition, and rhyme of poetry and verse help children predict what is coming next in the print.

Children make connections between letters and sounds when they see and hear them at the same time; that is, they learn phonics when they see patterns of letters and sounds repeated in poems and verse. Poetry helps reluctant or disabled or struggling readers, because there are not many words on a page. We say there is a lot of "white space" because the limited number of words leave open space on the page. The short lines of verse and the small number of words do not intimidate a child who struggles to read them.

Poetry Helps Children Learn to Write

When children write, they draw upon their knowledge of language. If their language storehouse is filled with a variety of words and concepts from many sources, they have a rich selection from which to draw. If they have heard others play with language sounds and meanings, they know that language is a plaything as well as a way to explain their world.

Poetry Helps Children Learn to Think

Poetry shows children new ways to view the world. It presents fresh perspectives on life and upends stereotyped ways of thinking. It helps readers to see new meanings as they consider the words of poetry.

Using Poetry in the Classroom

Poetry becomes the glue to bind groups of students and teachers together; it helps to create a community of learners. When students talk about their favorite poems, teachers gain insight about them by sharing the poems they choose. Just as reading together and talking about what we read develops a sense of community, so, too, does reading and talking about poetry.

Poetry is an oral art form. It doesn't live until it is read—or said—out loud. One day as we were working on the manuscript for this book, Marilyn read aloud Nikki

Reasons for Reading Poetry
. . . .
Reading poetry helps children to:
- discover poetry they like
- know where to find poems they like
- learn about what poets do
- learn how language works
- develop oral eloquence, reading fluency, and writing skills
- learn how poems work

Giovanni's "Kidnap Poem" from *Poems That Sing to You* (Strickland 1993). I was stunned. I had never "heard" that poem with the intonation and meaning Marilyn added through her voice, even though I had read the words on paper many times. For everyone, but especially for children, poetry comes alive when it's heard.

Getting Ready: Background Preparation for Poetry Teachers

Children learn from what surrounds them. If we immerse them in baseball, they learn about baseball. Not a single one of the players in the National Baseball League was born loving to play baseball. They each had somebody who put a ball into their hands, took them to a park or to Little League games, and played catch with them. Somebody tossed a ball to them over and over while they swung at it with a bat. Some of them even bought baseball uniform pajamas and baseball caps. They immersed children in baseball and the children learned to love baseball. If we immerse children in poetry, they will learn to love poetry.

Criteria for Selecting Poetry

Children like poems that:
- help them understand
- make them laugh, cry, or wonder
- help them see mental pictures (images)
- cause them to play with the sounds of language
- help them think about the world in a new way

Think about immersion the way Australian writer Mem Fox (1993) describes it. Using a plastic doll and a bucket of water, she plunges the doll deep into the water, and asks:

- If the water is Italian, will this child learn English? No! She'll learn Italian!

- If the water is a home without books, will this child be an avid reader? No! She'll probably be an avid watcher of television!

- If the water is a classroom in which the teacher bathes this child in good literature by reading aloud every day, will the child's reading and writing develop in leaps and bounds? Yes! (29)

Children learn what we immerse them in, especially poetry.

Immersing Your Students in Poetry

- Search for poetry—starting today. Look for anything that appeals to you. Copy poems you like into a notebook.

- Collect poems, posters, and books about upcoming class activities. Keep them close at hand and display them around the classroom.

- Watch for opportunities to use poetry related to any topic on any occasion. For example, turn to Lee Bennett Hopkins for holiday poems: *Beat the Drum: Independence Day Has Come* ([1977], 1993); *Easter Buds Are Springing* ([1979], 1993); *Good Morning to You, Valentine* ([1976], 1993);

Merrily Comes Our Harvest In: Poems for Thanksgiving ([1978], 1993). For history, look for Lee Bennett Hopkins, *Hand in Hand: American History in Poetry* (1995).

- Memorize some of your favorite poems. It doesn't need to be an entire poem, just a line or two that catches your fancy. Read them aloud until you know parts of them by heart. "Keep a poem in your pocket" for special moments in a classroom.

- Create displays, including poetry and book collections, for topics you study. The displays get students excited about what's coming, cause them to ask questions, and motivate them to find out about the topic.

- Alert your students to an upcoming event or study by asking *them* to find poems on the topic. Ask students to share what they find, then group the poems together on a bulletin board. Choose appropriate headings and categorize the poems under them.

Teachers' Checklist for Selecting Poetry

- Can children understand it? Can they understand it with help from adults?
- Does the poem stir emotions (delight, sadness, nostalgia)?
- Does it create images of sight, touch, smell, taste?
- Does it play with the sounds of language? Does the sound echo the sense?
- Does the rhythm reinforce the meaning?

- Collect specialized anthologies—poems by several poets on one subject. (For example, *Ragged Shadows: Poems of Halloween Night* collected by Lee Bennett Hopkins [1993] or *Weather Report* collected by Jane Yolen [1993b].)

- Collect generalized anthologies—by many poets on many subjects. (For example, *The Scott, Foresman Anthology of Children's Literature* by Zena Sutherland and Myra Cohn Livingston [1984] or *The Random House Book of Poetry* by Jack Prelutsky [1983].)

- Collect individualized anthologies—books containing the works of one poet. (For example, *Dogs and Dragons, Trees and Dreams* by Karla Kuskin [1980] or *The Reason for the Pelican* by John Ciardi [1994].) Keep the anthologies in the classroom for poetry searches on weather, holidays, families, places visited, topics studied, field trips, and special moments.

- Copy special poems onto large chart paper. If you can get them laminated or mounted on cardboard, they last longer.

- Place poem posters in library corners, classroom displays, block cities, housekeeping corners, play stores, and computer corners.

- File laminated poem posters in cartons partitioned into segments with cardboard dividers. Label sections according to poster content: Weather, Nonsense, Rhymes, Families, Halloween. You will have access to what you need at a moment's notice.

- Keep a variety of types of poetry on topics that appeal to your students. Students' tastes vary.

- Keep poetry alive in your classroom by seeking new voices as well as cherishing the old. Ask your school librarian to let you know about any new poetry books that come in—try to get them for your students. Take your students to the poetry section of the school and public library to sample read from the collections. Poetry is coded 811 in the Dewey Decimal System.

- Read professional journals that list and annotate the latest in poetry books for children. (For example, *Book Links, The Horn Book, School Library Journal, The Reading Teacher, Language Arts, The Bulletin of the Center for Children's Books,* and *The New Advocate.*)

- Acquaint your students with the works of award-winning poets. Collect the works of poets who won the National Council of Teachers of English Award for Poetry for Children: David McCord, Aileen Fisher, Karla Kuskin, Myra Cohn Livingston, Eve Merriam, John Ciardi, Lilian Moore, Arnold Adoff, Valerie Worth, and Barbara Esbensen. Surround your students with books by these poets. Children should be exposed to the best examples of beautiful language we can find.

- Consult your students, your own children, and your colleagues about their favorite poems. Their recommendations are worthwhile.

PART ONE

Developing a Love of Poetry

Language Arts, Reading, Writing, and Poetry

When I taught elementary school, I began each day with poetry and verse. For the primary grades I often used poems by A.A. Milne about John putting his great big waterproof boots on (as in "Happiness" in Milne's *When We Were Very Young* [1924]) or Christopher Robin finding a beetle he named Alexander (in "Forgiven" in Milne's *Now We Are Six* [1927]). The children would chime in quickly to say the verses along with me, rapidly memorizing their favorites. I soon turned poetry time over to them by asking, "Who wants to choose the next one?" An eager poetry lover always had a poem ready to suggest.

As I reflect on my teaching, I realize that I am establishing the basic conditions that facilitate language learning (Cambourne 1987): I *immerse* them in poetry; I *model* how it is said and *demonstrate* how much fun it is; I *accept their approximations* or *attempts* to say poems; and I provide lots of *opportunities for practice* by doing it every day. Children learn to love poetry just as they learn to love language because it increases their control over their world and gives them joy and laughter. Their quick, enthusiastic response illustrates the old axiom "We get good at what we do." The more poetry they hear, the more they learn. The more they learn, the more they love it.

The strategies that follow: Browsing Through Poetry; Building Anthologies; Warm-Ups; Celebrate Poetry; Poetry to Enrich Stories; Poetry for Beginning Readers; A Gift of Poetry; and Poetry for Students with Special Needs are ways to surround children with poetry in classrooms. If we first develop a love of poetry in our students, then they will be ready and eager to learn about it and from it later on.

Browsing Through Poetry

In order to have children reach for poetry books with as much enthusiasm as they reach for other books, we must teach them to browse through poetry. They don't go to a library and pick up just any book on the shelf expecting to like it. They listen to books read aloud, they sample read (taste test), they talk with their friends, and they begin to create a list of favorite authors, illustrators, and genres that appeal to them—fiction, informational books, mystery, or humor. If we want children to develop a love of poetry, we must help them become familiar with a variety of poets and styles. When we do this, children learn how to look through books to find poems they like, they learn how to sample read, they begin to recognize certain poets' work, and they develop a personal taste in poetry. They can begin to build their personal anthologies of poems they like.

Looking at Poetry

Marilyn: When a colleague asks me to do a poetry reading-writing workshop with her, we first collect lots of poetry books. We gather them from her classroom, my library, the school library, and the public library. We invite students to bring in poetry books they own. The end result is stacks of books piled on tables surrounding students in the classroom.

Before we ask students to devote time browsing, the co-teacher and I talk with the students about the books and read selected poems aloud. We handle some books as treasured possessions, some as mysterious objects to explore, and some as interesting curiosities. The books vary; they contain humorous, serious, short, and long poems. Some books focus on a particular theme, some are multicultural, some are on differing topics, some are picture books, some are general anthologies. Some contain poems by a single poet; some have poems by numerous poets.

We give the students about an hour to browse through the books, explaining that at the end of the hour they should have a poem they *really like* to read to their classmates. The teacher and I circulate among the students, leading some to books they might like and keeping other students on task. Here are some poems they usually choose: "How to Eat a Poem" (Merriam 1964); "Sick" (Silverstein 1974); "Heartland" (Siebert 1989); and "The Cardinal" (Yolen 1990).

Students type the poems they choose on computers or copy them in their own handwriting, making sure to cite the author, the title of the book, and the publisher. Most of the poems they choose have rhyme and most involve humor. A few poem choices are serious and a few tell a story. All hold the attention of the class as we practice reading the poems to each other. This takes several days. During the sharing sessions, children most often read the poem they chose themselves, but sometimes others want to read it, too. When Nick says, "Hey, let me see that one," he passes on an unspoken compliment to his friend.

....

Encouraging Poetry Browsing

- Provide a variety of poetry books and ask students to choose a poem they like.

- Model reading poems aloud, then have students read their favorites to classmates. Work in pairs, small groups, or whole groups. Use solo reading, choral reading, readers theatre, or another interactive reading plan.

- Ask every person in the class to choose a favorite poem from a single anthology to expose students to different themes and styles.

- Give students a specific purpose in selecting a poem. For example, choose a poem that pictures vividly the Jamaican island culture in *Not a Copper Penny in Me House,* by Monica Gunning (1993); choose a poem reminiscent of a favorite song from *Poems That Sing to You,* collected by Michael Strickland (1993); choose an appropriate rainy, snowy, cloudy, or foggy day poem from *Weather Report,* collected by Jane Yolen (1993b), to form part of a class poetry weather report; choose a poem that expresses how you feel; choose a poem that relates to a classroom topic of study.

....

STRATEGY 2
Building Anthologies

Peer recommendations are powerful motivators. When a classmate chooses a favorite poem, the choice is contagious. Just being part of a group scrambling to write down a favorite poem from the chalkboard builds a certain kind of eagerness. Enthusiasm for poetry is worth a little bit of controlled chaos.

Marilyn: After the browsing session, the next part is chaotic but fun. We hang up all the poems chosen during browsing on the bulletin board or chalkboard. Children walk around the room to read the poems and to decide which ones they want for their personal anthologies. The classroom buzzes with excitement and noise during this time. They know what they want. They remember certain poems from the sharing session and ask for them if they cannot find them. They talk to a friend and go back to look for more.

A few days later, our individual anthologies are born. The spirit of poetry is contagious; in a class of twenty-two students every student has written down at least sixteen poems.

I always learn something about the students through the poems they choose. One very active boy tends in his reading and writing to edge toward violence, partly out of interest and curiosity, but partly for the shock value it brings from the teacher and the class. Here, though, he chooses a very gentle, quiet poem about crickets in the tall grass:

Crickets

Crickets
Talk
In the tall
Grass
All
Late summer
Long.
When
Summer
Is gone,
The dry
Grass
Whispers
Alone.

—Valerie Worth (in *Small Poems* [1987b])

Another boy who usually appears cynical chooses a poem that reveals an interest in the study of Native Americans that previously has gone undetected. A serious, studious girl picks a poem rollicking with humor, which shows the class another side of her personality. Poetry preferences reveal information about students that we may discover in no other way. Knowing the poems children like helps us to enrich their learning in many ways.

*Helping Students
Build Anthologies*

- Have students share their choices and write down their favorite poems.

- Make anthologies a source of pride and pleasure. Refer to them often and keep eyes alert for additions.

- Start autograph books as a fad among your students. Encourage students to write verses in each other's books.

S T R A T E G Y   3
Warm-Ups

Poetry is meant to be read aloud. Students who hear it as a natural part of every day incorporate it into their language and their lives.

Ginnie: My third graders gather eagerly each morning in the corner of the room where there is an area rug and a chart stand next to my chair. Their faces contain the same expressions you expect to see when a stack of birthday presents await opening. They don't know exactly what's coming, but they know they're going to like it!

    I choose a poem or song related to the weather, something that has happened in class, or an event that is just around the corner. I introduce the new poem or song. We explore it together, have fun with the rhythm and rhyme of it, then move on to other favorites from other days. Children make requests, and everyone joins in with the reading. For about fifteen minutes, the class unites in the joyful sounds of poetry and song. I call this time "Warm-Ups," and I believe that our school day is just not the same without it; the children feel the same way.

*Morning Circle
Poetry Time*

Starting the Day

- Select a poem. Choose one with a strong beat, catchy phrasing, and strong feeling, such as "Lewis Has a Trumpet," by Karla Kuskin (Strickland 1993), or "Days," by Karle Wilson Baker (Goldstein 1992). Let the age and experience of your students guide your choice. Copy the poem onto chart paper or poster board.

- Display the poem where the children can see it. Rehearse the poem aloud to yourself before you share it with students. Read it several ways to see the different effects you can achieve. When you feel comfortable with the style you've chosen, you're ready!

- Read the poem aloud to the class. Then point to the beginning of each line while you ask students to read along with you. Or, read it to them while they keep their eyes closed, so they can concentrate on the music of the words.

- Read it aloud again. The poet Eve Merriam advises reading a poem twice so that the words and the music of the words can be heard.

- On the second or third reading, invite volunteers to read with you. Repeat the invitation until everyone who wants to read has had a turn. Be sensitive to shy children and insecure readers—they feel more comfortable reading along with a group rather than reading alone.

- Invite all of the children to read together. Work toward unity of expression; the sound of one voice. The children may have different interpretations about the way a poem should be read. That's fine. Let others hear the differences, and ask for explanations about suggested changes. Try their ideas as a group.

- Ask the children: What did we do with our voices? How does that sound to you? Where did we read slowly? Quickly? Loudly? Softly? Where did we stop or pause? Why? What did we do at the end of a line? Why do you think we read the poem that way? Do you think this poem would sound better if it were read by just one person, or by many? Why do you think so?

- Finish with: Let's try it.

. . . .

STRATEGY   4
Celebrate Poetry

Celebrate poetry every day. Start morning circle with poetry, and have poetry breaks. Establish poetry circles celebrating the poetry students write as well as the poetry they read and choose as favorites.

Ginnie: When students begin to write their own poems, I often see poetry become the breakthrough for reluctant authors, as well as the stretch
that more able writers need. I recognize each child's effort. For some, finding the topic is the most difficult part. For others, learning how to edit and
pare away unnecessary words is a struggle. I let all of the children know
that the effort is well worth it. We cherish our classroom anthologies. We
devote entire bulletin boards to our poetry. And we celebrate our work by
sharing it out loud. Here is one poem we like to read together:

Poems

A poem is a magical boat to ride
in a sea of words with a rhyming tide.
It takes us from some hum-drum shore
to places we never have been before—
shimmering islands of sensation
captured by imagination.
New lands wait for us to sight,
so climb aboard! The wind is right.
Rocking rhythms will take us along
to the rising crest of a noteless song.

—Bobbi Katz (Goldstein 1992)

Poetry reflects life—our everyday events and our feelings about them.
When students realize that poetry mirrors life, they also realize that every
event is important enough to explore in writing. The more they explore
through poetry, the closer they look at ordinary events. That gives them
confidence to reach into the unknown.

Enjoying Poetry

- Celebrate poetry every day.

- Establish poetry circles in which students meet to read aloud, share,
  and talk about poems they find and poems they write. These can be
  similar to "literature circles," as described by Harste, Short, and Burke
  (1988).

- Frame poems students write and mount them on bulletin boards or
  walls.

- Use student poems as models when exploring new poetry forms.

- Have poetry readings. Invite parents, groups of students, administra-
  tors, school board members, local citizens, and news reporters to listen
  to students read their poems aloud.

- Help students to become critics of their own work as they develop anthologies of their own poetry. Ask them to select the "best" they have written over a period of time. Then acknowledge it in some way. For example: Enter it in a contest. Frame it and hang it in the classroom. Give it as a gift to someone special. Have a "read aloud" of favorite poems at a poetry tea or a classroom share. Illustrate a poem, then mount the poem and picture together on colored tag board. Display illustrated poems in the hallway, trophy case, principal's office, cafeteria, or teachers' lounge. Publish poems in a classroom or school newspaper. Submit poems to the local newspaper with a description of school events and human interest items about the authors.

- Help students see the many reasons to celebrate their poetry. Show them the relationships between thinking and writing poetry about an event or an object by reminding them that they are problem solving, researching, questioning, observing, and giving factual information through their poetry. These are higher-level thinking skills that good citizens and good students need.

- Celebrate the poems students memorize. Third-grade students learned a new verse of Maurice Sendak's *Chicken Soup with Rice* (1986) each month, doubling up on the last few to include months we were not in session. By the end of the school year, every child knew the entire poem by heart. Were they ever proud! Every visitor to the classroom was invited to listen to them recite it.

....

S T R A T E G Y   5

Poetry to Enrich Stories

When reading a story aloud to a group of students—or teachers—find a poem to accompany it. Look for a poem that captures the essence of the experience, extends the story, or crystallizes its meaning. Poetry enriches the story experience and makes it memorable because it magnifies an emotional response. Poems heighten our emotions and help us become more sensitive to an idea.

Ginnie: When I read a story aloud, I find poems to match the theme or feeling of the book. One day I read *Chrysanthemum* by Kevin Henkes (1991), a story about a mouse child who thinks her name is absolutely perfect—until she goes to school and her schoolmates make fun of it. I then read several poems about children's names. The following one heightens students' feelings about names.

And Off He Went Just as Proud as You Please

Said Billy to Willy,
"You have a silly name!"
Said Willy to Billy,
"Our names are much the same."

Said Billy to Willy,
"That is not true.
Your name is silly,
Just like you.

"Your name's a silly shame.
My name is fine.
For my name, my name,
My name is *mine!*"

—John Ciardi (Ciardi 1991b)

A poem by Lee Bennett Hopkins (Hopkins 1974) shows what mothers think about their children's writing:

My Name

I wrote my name on the sidewalk
But the rain washed it away.

I wrote my name on my hand
But the soap washed it away.

I wrote my name on the birthday card
I gave to Mother today

And there it will stay
For Mother never throws
ANYTHING
of mine away!

By calling attention to similar themes in poetry and other forms of literature, you help students become aware of more connections. Their literary understanding grows.

- Encourage students to associate poetry with picture books or novels. During poetry or book discussions, talk about how we identify with a character's emotions. As students share moments from their own lives that mirror episodes or emotions from books, they begin to recognize the common elements of what it means to be human. Ask students to search for poems that remind them of a character or story event. Poems that reflect our emotions deepen our response to literature.

- Model connections between poems and books. For example, when reading *Is Your Mama a Llama?* by Deborah Guarino (1989), read "The Llama Who Had No Pajama" by Mary Ann Hoberman (Hoberman 1981). When reading *A Chair for My Mother* by Vera Williams (1983), read poems from *Families* by Dorothy and Michael Strickland (1994), as well as ones from *Fathers, Mothers, Sisters, Brothers* by Mary Ann Hoberman (1991). When reading *The Little Fir Tree* by Margaret Wise Brown (1979), read e. e. cummings's *Little Tree* (1987). When reading Jean Little's book, *Kate* (1971), read the poem "Writers," from *Hey, World, Here I Am!* also by Jean Little (1989).

- Have students write in response journals when they read books. Sometimes their response may be a poem. Here is a sixth grader's response journal entry after she read *Where the Red Fern Grows* by Wilson Rawls (1961).

The Beautiful Sunrise

Sitting on the mountain by myself
for the first time
waiting for the sun to rise
to start a new day.
Thinking about the day my dogs died.
The first time I saw them
I thought I would be with them forever,
but one died because of a Mountain Lion
and the other one died because she loved that old dog,
    her brother.
Their names were Old Dan and Little Ann.
I will never forget their faces when I first got them.
And the night they first treed a 'coon.
And when they won the gold cup.
And risked their lives for me that night
and the reason they died . . .
        because they loved me.

—Candace

- Explore the various themes and viewpoints expressed in the books your students read. Ask students to explain why they think prejudice, or growing up, or courage is a theme in a book. Discuss the notion of multiple themes in a book. Some children may clearly recognize one theme but be unable to see another unless it is brought out through sharing so they can relate it to their own experiences. Candace's poem about *Where the Red Fern Grows* is as much about her fears of losing her own dog as it is about the book character's.

- Encourage students to turn prose into poetry by exploring their written responses for words and phrases that seem especially vivid and meaningful. Help them revise these snippets of language into a poem by choosing more colorful vocabulary; deleting unnecessary words; switching phrases around; and adding thoughts to fill in gaps in meaning, rhythm, or sequence. Show them how poets carefully arrange words on paper to appeal to the eye and to attract the reader's mind.

- Use examples of student language from their response journals or book talks to begin a group poem about a book, a character, or a theme. Help students to identify poetic phrases and words in their own writing. Work as a group to model turning prose language into poetry. For example, one day Ginnie's students looked back through their response journals after reading Katherine Paterson's *The Great Gilly Hopkins* (1978). Cheryl found a statement she had written with great passion: "I hated it when Gilly went with her grandmother instead of going back to Trotter because she had just gotten used to living with Trotter and besides her mother wasn't going to be around anyhow." The group worked together to cut away unnecessary words and keep the essence of Cheryl's feelings. Here is the poem the group chose after rearranging the words in several different ways:

> Gilly Hopkins
> stayed with Grandma
> 'Stead of Mame Trotter.
> Didn't want to
> But did it anyway.
> Knew that Grandma
> Needed her most
> 'Cause Courtney Rutherford Hopkins
> Wasn't coming home.

STRATEGY 6
Poetry for Beginning Readers

Some books are easier than others for children to learn to read from be-cause the words are predictable; children can predict what the words will say. Features that make a book predictable include rhythmic (melodic) lan-guage, rhyming words, repeated words (vocabulary), and patterned sto-ries. Beginning readers gain confidence in their ability to decode print by reading predictable texts. And, as they gain experience in decoding, they develop fluency in reading. Predictable texts are developmentally appro-priate material for beginning readers.

Figuring Out the Code

Ginnie: When I'm teaching a group of preprimary-grade children, po-etry and verse come to my rescue. Most of these children don't recognize the letters of the alphabet. They don't know Mother Goose rhymes. They can't write their names. The diagnostic procedures I use indicate that the children are not ready for direct reading instruction. Often they have little interest in reading, although they are well schooled in TV.

I put aside all the regular reading instruction books and collect a vari-ety of picture books, ABC books, counting books, Mother Goose and nursery rhymes, and poetry. I copy rhymes on to posters, I collect Big Books, and I hang charts filled with verses all around the classroom. I lit-erally saturate the children in print. In this way, I use poetry and stories for reading in-struction without destroying their beauty. For example, when I introduce a new book, I read the story or poem with enthusiasm and let its dramatic impact sink in. Later, we look care-fully at the words and the letters.

We chant verses together, we sing songs to-gether, and we say favorite lines together. The children listen to books on tape. They continu-ally "read and pretend read" books to each other, and they look at books together. They of-ten read verses on the charts and point to words they know. Through all the chanting and read-ing together, they are getting the cadence of reading. Through all the pointing and following

Poetry for Beginning Readers

Children learning to read a text need certain qualities that support their efforts to decode print. Poetry has several features that help young readers to figure out the code:

- words that rhyme
- words that begin with the same sound
- words that end with the same sound
- predictable words
- patterned phrases
- a small number of words on a page
- words that sound like natural language
- phrase-structured text—a complete phrase on one line

along, they are making connections between the words they see and the words they say. They begin to figure out the code. Gradually, they become readers.

I also use the Big Book version of *The Gingerbread Boy* (Galdone 1983) with its repetitive phrase, "Run, run as fast as you can/ You can't catch me/ I'm the gingerbread man." I show the children the cover and ask, "What do you see?" I write their observations on chart paper, and put the children's names beside their comments. I give them time to predict what might happen in the story and urge them to ask questions the story might answer. Then I read the story all the way through. Later we check to see which of their predictions are close. The children find their own responses on the chart and read them aloud to decide which ones have been confirmed by the story. Then I read the story aloud again, pausing for comments and opinions.

Later, I read the story and repetitive verse aloud a third time. When I come to a part I think most children will remember, I pause and let the children fill in the words orally. Some fill in from memory, but some actually focus on the page, following my pointer as I run it below the words.

I turn the story into a cloze procedure by covering up predictable words in the text with Post-its and having the children guess what words are under them. I turn the reading over to a child by giving her the pointer and having her lead the group in reading aloud. The children are now early readers.

David Harrison's poem "My Book!" (Harrison 1993) expresses the way they feel.

I did it!
I did it!
Come and look
At what I've done!
I read a book!
When someone wrote it

Books for Beginning Readers

Here are some easy-to-read poetic texts:

Brown Bear, Brown Bear, What Do You See? by Bill Martin, Jr., 1983.
Bunches & Bunches of Bunnies by Louise Mathews, 1978.
Catch Me and Kiss Me and Say It Again by Clyde Watson, 1978.
Chicken Soup with Rice by Maurice Sendak, 1986.
Each Peach Pear Plum by Janet and Allan Ahlberg, 1979.
The Gingerbread Boy by Paul Galdone, 1983.
I Know an Old Lady Who Swallowed a Fly by Nadine B. Westcott, 1980.
If All the Seas Were One Sea by Janina Domanska, 1987.
Jane Yolen's Old MacDonald Songbook by Jane Yolen, 1994a.
Jesse Bear, What Will You Wear? by Nancy White Carlstrom, 1986.
Mary Wore Her Red Dress & Henry Wore His Green Sneakers by Merle Peek, 1988.
More Surprises by Lee Bennett Hopkins, 1987.
New Baby Calf by Edith N. Chase, 1986.
On Market Street by Arnold Lobel, 1981.
Over in the Meadow by Paul Galdone, 1986a.
Over in the Meadow: A Counting-Out Rhyme by Olivia A. Wadsworth and Mary M. Rae, 1985.
Polar Bear, Polar Bear, What Do You Hear? by Bill Martin, Jr., 1991.
A Rose in My Garden by Arnold Lobel, 1984.
Seven Little Rabbits by John Becker, 1985.
Singing Bee! by Jane Hart, 1982.
Soap Soup by Karla Kuskin, 1992.
Something's Sleeping in the Hall by Karla Kuskin, 1985.
Surprises by Lee Bennett Hopkins, 1984.
Three Little Kittens by Paul Galdone, 1986b.
Tomie de Paola's Mother Goose by Tomie de Paola, 1985.

Long ago
For me to read,
How did he know
That this was the book
I'd take from the shelf
And lie on the floor
And read by myself?
I really read it!
Just like that!
Word by word,
From first to last!
I'm sleeping with
This book in bed,
This first FIRST book
I've ever read!

Helping Beginning Readers

- Collect poems for beginning readers.

- Write out song lyrics and simple verses that students know by heart. Help them make their own books of songs and rhymes.

- Search for predictable books so that students can figure out what is coming next in print.

- Ask students to search for books they can read. Build a classroom collection of predictable, easy-to-read books.

STRATEGY 7

A Gift of Poetry

A gift of poetry can be opened again and again. Give children a gift that can last a lifetime—a love of poetry.

Giving the Gift of Poetry

Marilyn: When my daughter was in elementary school, she discovered that she liked the poetry of Langston Hughes. For her birthday, I typed out several of his dream poems and put them into a booklet cut in the shape of a cloud. I loved the idea that we shared his poetry together. Months later, I received a poetry gift from her. In newly learned calligraphy, she wrote out

"Keep a Poem in Your Pocket" by Beatrice Schenk de Regniers (Prelutsky 1983). She labeled this "for the gift of dream poems," and included a poem about maps "for the wonderful trips you've taken us on!"

As a mother, I see beauty in the beginnings of our gifts of poetry to each other—in poems, songs, or in moments. As a teacher, I realize that my daughter is browsing through poetry books to find poems that have special meaning and connections for us. And as she copies the poetic language, she is absorbing the wonder of poetry. Poems become gifts that capture moments and memories.

Later, I carry the idea of poetry gifts to school. I have a student, Linda, who is seriously below grade level in reading and who has a low tolerance for reading whole stories. But when the reading is a poem—with all that meaning, short lines (sparse text), and white space—she is hooked. Our reading begins and progresses with poetry. The repetition, rhythm, and controlled vocabulary minimize the risk of reading, giving Linda more patience and allowing her to discover the strategies that good readers use. Linda corrects herself more easily while reading poetry, so miscues no longer stop her reading flow. I frequently give her poems "to keep in her pocket." I know she reads them at home and collects them. Sometimes I write a poem for her and occasionally she writes one for me. We develop rapport as we develop reading skills. Not a word needs to be said when we read "Things" from *Honey, I Love* (Greenfield 1978). We just smile.

Things

Went to the corner
Walked in the store
Bought me some candy
Ain't got it no more
Ain't got it no more

Went to the beach
Played on the shore
Built me a sandhouse
Ain't got it no more
Ain't got it no more

Went to the kitchen
Lay down on the floor
Made me a poem
Still got it
Still got it

—Eloise Greenfield

Another child, Candace, expresses her feelings about frogs in her poem (see Figure 1).

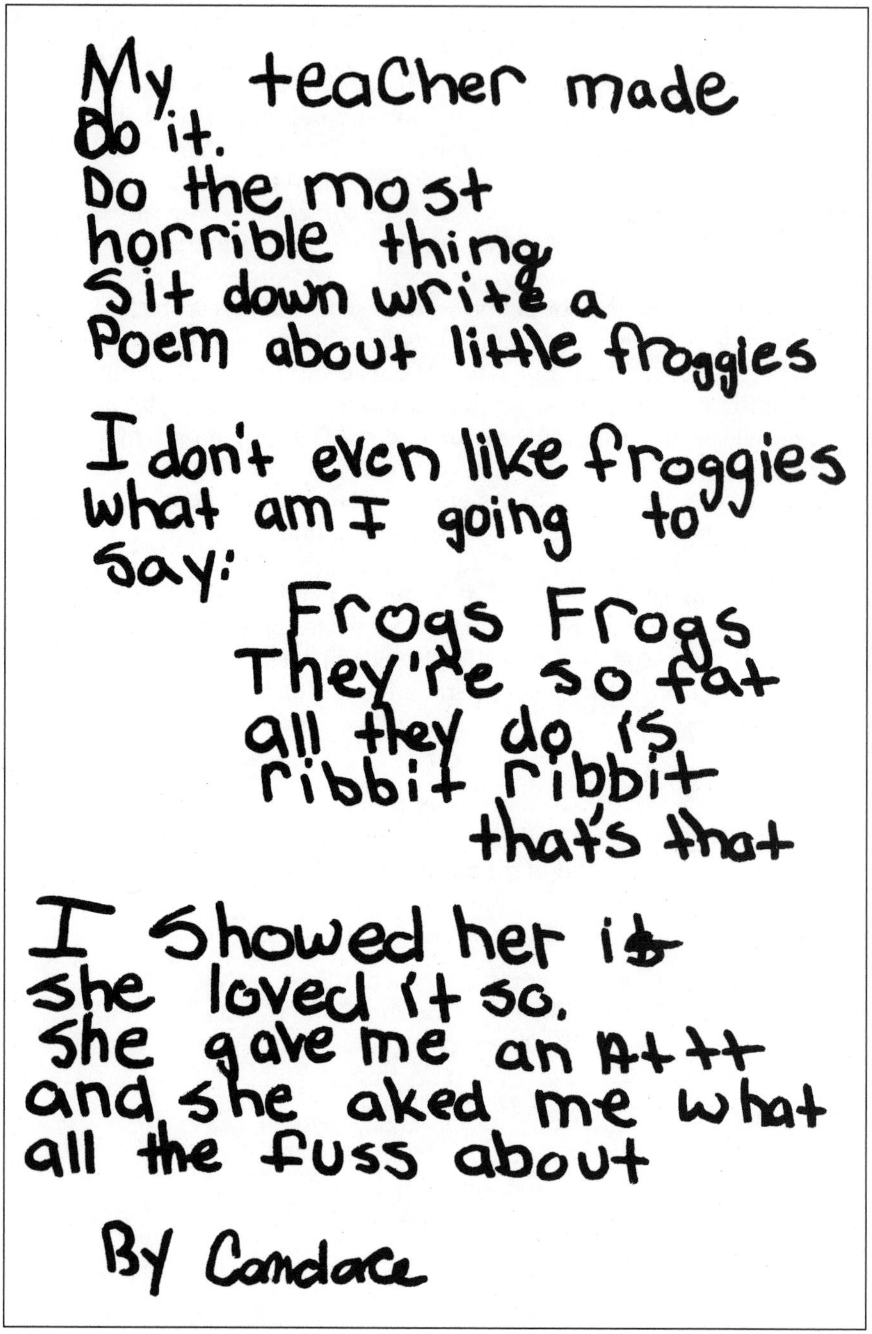

My   teaCher made
Do it.
Do the most
horrible thing
Sit down write a
Poem about little froggies

I don't even like froggies
what am I going   to
Say:
            Frogs Frogs
        They're so fat
        all they do is
        ribbit ribbit
                    that's that

I Showed her it
she loved it so.
She gave me an A+++
and she aked me what
all the fuss about

    By Candace

FIGURE 1. Candace's poem about frogs.

Linda and Candace are two of hundreds of my students with special needs who respond to poetry. Through a love of poetry, many students with learning problems begin to write and to make their voices clear. Although we may be able to spot LD students as readers, their poetic voices are as strong and as accomplished as their peers.

- Start a poetry gift exchange. As a group, look through poetry collections to find poems that remind you of yourself or someone else. Talk to your students about what you are thinking as you select a poem and consider whether it is appropriate for the person you have in mind. Discuss the choices you make. Model matching poems with people by giving poems to your students, and have them find poems to exchange. Give a child who loves skiing a snow poem. Give a child who loves horses a poem from Nancy Springer's *Music of Their Hooves* (1994). Give musical students "Lewis Has a Trumpet" or "Practice" from *Poems That Sing To You* by Michael Strickland (1993).

- Create a bulletin board for items of interest—newspaper articles, reminders, and poetry. Encourage students to scan the board for information as well as for new poems for their anthologies.

- Illustrate a poem. Frame it for a desk, the wall, or a gift.

- Exchange poems with friends in lieu of gifts. A high school friend and I had exchanged holiday gifts for years. Recently, I suggested that we give each other a poem instead.

STRATEGY 8
Poetry for Students with Special Needs

Special needs students are increasingly being included in regular classrooms for major portions of their academic program. Poetry can be both a stimulant and an equalizer in bridging the gap between achievement level and grade level. Poetry appeals to children who have varied learning styles and achievement levels, or ones who come from various grade levels and ability groups. Poetry puts children of differing abilities on equal footing.

Marilyn: As a special education teacher, I spend much of my day working with another teacher in a regular classroom. One of the first activities I include my students with special needs in is writers workshop. Learning-disabled and at-risk students have experienced failure more often than their counterparts, and probably have developed their off-task behaviors to a larger extent, too. But writers workshop is a relaxed time in the classroom where students do not need to fear being called upon for answers they don't know. It is a time for individuals to write from their own experiences and a time for them to join peers to conference in the corner of the room. If students need help, teachers are available for ideas or suggestions.

In a fourth-grade classroom during writing workshop, we start our immersion in poetry by looking through books for poems to share with classmates. I have several resource room children in this class. Because poems can be short but powerful and can be easy to read but wonderful, the learning-disabled students are at no disadvantage here. The regular classroom teacher and I help all of the children browse through books until everyone finds a poem to share. The students copy the poems they like, share the poems, sign up for ones they want to copy, and then we have the beginnings of our personal anthologies.

Poetry appeals to Andrew, a student with special needs. It helps him to feel competent in his individual endeavors; he likes to feel equal when he is a member of a group. When I see him in the hallway, he asks me when writing workshop will be held so he can make sure it is in his schedule. He is taking initiative in a new way, planning his time, finding a poem to share, bringing his anthology folder on time, and writing a poem of his own that he truly likes. Here is a poem Andrew wrote:

> Grown-ups are funny,
> full of fun
> because we laugh.
> I like when
> they make a mistake.
> Grown-ups teach us
> things that we
> never heard of.

Poetry helps nonfluent readers to become more fluent. It is fun to read and reread, and rereading promotes fluency. Poems can be short with lots of white space on a page and still be considered respectable reading material for higher grade levels.

Like Andrew, Naquon and David became as interested in writing poetry as they were in reading it. Naquon wrote the following poem, called "In the City."

It was one hot blazing
Memorial Day
I wished it were
the Fourth of July
I wanted to see
the fireworks
sparkle over the
Statue of Liberty

That day I
went to the
Empire State Building
when I looked down
I felt like
I was going
to fall off
Then I went
to the subway
where I saw
a man playing
the saxophone

At Central Park
I went under
the bridge
that Kevin walked
under in the movie
"Home Alone Two"
and I walked
around the whole
park twice
I got tired
of all the walking
but it was
A wonderful
Memorial Day.

—Naquon

David wrote this poem, called "Dream World."

Every person has a dream world all of their own
    That they are king of.
Some are deserted,
    Some are packed.

> Some are in the future.
>   Some are in the past.
> There you are eternal
>   Where you cannot be harmed.
> Some people have two.
>   Others have three.
> But I have infinity and they're all for me.

Success breeds success. When we ask children with special needs to read their anthology at night instead of thirty pages of a chapter book, they are much more willing. They can do it alone. There are choices. They can read favorite poems first. They can read the easy poems first. They can skip around. Before long, I find that the reluctant readers are much more fluent when they read chapter books with me. I believe that developing the feeling of fluency in students has as important a place in remedial reading as phonics, structural analysis, and authenticity. And it starts with poems.

Increasing Fluency in Students with Special Needs

- Ask special needs students to collect poems they like. Put them in an individual anthology to read and re-read.

- Encourage students to share poems by reading them aloud to classmates and parents.

- Ask students to check their predictions against graphophonic information in the text. For example, in *Did You Ever See?* (Einsel 1962), the phrase "Did you ever see a crow?" is paired with a sentence ending with a rhyming word. Ask students to suggest what the word might be, then check to see which word the poet chose. Write poems from this model.

- Copy the words from a poem or a predictable story onto sentence strips, then laminate them. Give them to students to place in the correct order.

- Have students regenerate a text. Prepare a copy of a familiar nursery rhyme but leave blanks for the students to complete.

- Extend the pattern of a predictable book. For example, after reading in Brian Wildsmith's book, *Cat on the Mat* (1982), have students continue the pattern by showing other animals that try to chase the cat off the mat.

PART TWO

Discovering How Poetry Works

Learn About Poetry

Children gradually build a background knowledge of what poetry is and how poems work as they read and write lots of poetry. It is more important for us to help them discover the joy of poetry than to check on their comprehension of the content of poems or their knowledge of poetic techniques. Little by little, they will develop an understanding of forms. It is more important for students to understand how to use the elements of poetry, such as sound, rhythm, and meaning, than to be able to define and identify the conventional poetic forms (Benton and Fox 1985).

Poetry forms are like a catch-22: if you start explaining and analyzing them, you're sure to turn kids off. However, as Sam Sebesta notes (Booth and Moore 1988), "unless you pay some attention to the technical side of poetry you're unlikely to know the full range of poetry's domains. In such instances, appreciation stops short of feeling the power of the poet's language, and you are likely to miss opportunities for bringing a poem to life" (74). This plan leads down a narrow path that calls for balance and good judgment about what to teach and when to teach it. The best—but hard to follow—advice is to make information about forms available as students need it.

Many of us grew to dislike poetry when we were forced to analyze poems—taking them apart and leaving them in shreds on the classroom floor. Others turned against poetry when we tried to write it but were required to learn about and follow rhythm patterns, such as iambic pentameter or dactyllic dimeter. It seems there were so many rules that we became lost in them, leaving the poems along the wayside.

Forget about teaching definitions and poetic forms at first. Don't try to teach concepts about form and pattern until children have had lots of experience and are comfortable with poems. They will let you know when they are ready for more information. When a child notices that a poem on the chalkboard has a rhyming pattern, he may say, "Hey, that rhymes." Then you can say, "Where does it rhyme? Show me." Once identified, you can give the pattern a name: "Yes, poets call that a couplet, *abab*, as in 'Sipping once, sipping twice, sipping chicken soup with rice.'" You can also show the pattern of *aabb* in "One, two,/ Buckle my shoe."

When your students are ready, show them that poems happen by design, not by accident. Conventional or traditional forms were developed over hundreds of years probably because poems were meant to be recited from memory and performed; the pattern helped people to memorize them. The cinquain, haiku, limerick, and ballad, for example, have rather clearly defined rules because they have been used for so long. One argument for using conventional or fixed forms is that they provide a discipline or challenge for the poet. Upper elementary students enjoy this challenge, too!

Just before St. Patrick's Day, for example, Ginnie hands out pages filled with limericks. Children read over them and laugh together. The form is contagious and one student, Larry, cannot resist it. He begins writing a limerick and will not let it go; he is determined to master it. After watching him struggle for several days to get his limerick just right, Ginnie suggests that he try free verse instead. But Larry is determined and eventually manages to get the meter right—with huge delight.

Modern poets often *create* a form that is uniquely appropriate to the content or experience of a particular piece. We call these open forms. Open forms have a way of crossing lines and slipping out of definitional boxes. One example, a concrete (shape) poem, is written in a shape to suggest its subject. When you show students a form, talk about it and help them experiment with it (see Figure 2). Let them know that it is available for them to use.

STRATEGY   9

Discovering the Elements of Poetry

Some teachers may be reluctant to use poetry in their classrooms because they feel that they don't know enough about it. Maybe they were intimidated by a college professor who used big words or other definitions, such

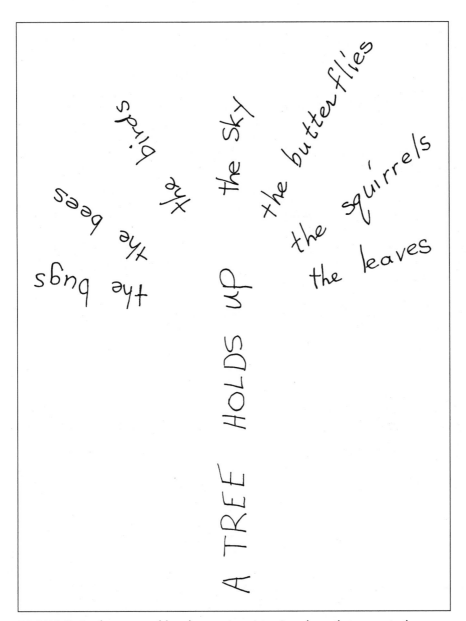

FIGURE 2. A concrete (shape) poem is written in a shape that suggests the subject of the poem.

as *iambic pentameter* or *trochee,* that they did not understand. It is not necessary to use all of the technical language to build a love of poetry and help students to discover it from the inside out. In fact, moving too quickly to use such terms may kill the poetry flower before it blossoms.

Sticking to a few simple concepts may be useful when students are trying to write poetry. For example, note that poets use a narrative voice to tell a story, and a lyrical voice to express their feelings about something or establish a mood. The dramatic voice has at least three recognizable types that you can discuss with students: the apostrophe (talking to things that cannot answer); the mask (pretending to be something else); and conversations (hearing a dialogue between two voices). See the glossary for other definitions.

All language has rhythm, but the rhythm in poetry is more pronounced—sometimes exaggerated. Rhythm is part of the unique characteristics of poetry. If students want to explore metrics (counting the beat), then help them define and find examples of different feet: iamb, trochee, anapest, and dactyl.

Poetry also uses lots of figurative language, such as simile, metaphor, and personification. It is better for students to discover the meanings of these elements for their own writing or reading needs than to have them taught didactically or simply because they appear in a syllabus or curriculum guide.

Poets manipulate elements of sound, rhythm, and meaning to create a powerful impact and to make words memorable. They call attention to language by using alliteration (repetition of initial consonants), assonance (repetition of vowel sounds at close intervals), onomatopoeia (words that sound like their meaning), and rhyme (words that sound alike). Poets condense meaning; they pack poetry with meaning. Lilian Moore says poetry should be like fireworks, packed carefully and artfully, ready to explode with unpredictable effects.

Working with Repetition

Ginnie: I begin writers workshop by reading aloud several poems that use repetition for rhythm's sake and to rivet our attention. I show words and phrases repeated for effect, as they appear in "Where We Ride To" from *Music of Their Hooves* (Springer 1994) and "My Daddy" by Eloise Greenfield (Strickland 1993). I use Christina Rossetti's "Who Has Seen the Wind?" (Yolen 1993b) as an example of repetition that makes the reader pause to think—we want to answer the question before we read further.

I show students how poets use repetition to make words memorable. I suggest they ask themselves: "Was the action I am writing about repeated more than once? Does a puppy wag its tail just one time? If it is an important action, how can I use repetition to show it?"

- Collect and share poems that play with language. When you read aloud poems with onomatopoeia and alliteration, explain the terms to students. Talk about how poets use the techniques to enhance the poem and our enjoyment of it.

- Create a class list of words that illustrate onomatopoeia, like *ooze, slither, sigh, slush, blubber,* and *trickle.* Keep the list posted so students can add to it and use it in their writing. ("Sound of Water" by Mary O'Neill [Paladino 1993] contains good examples of onomatopoeia.)

- Develop some of the words from the list into phrases and sentences. How could they be used in a poem. Ask for "sound" words that might be used in poems about music, a farm, machinery, or animals. This helps students to think about the language they use every day in a new way, and they begin to read, write, and listen with greater sensitivity.

- Share examples of alliteration with students. Poems such as "The Pickety Fence" by David McCord (Cullinan 1995); the Mother Goose verse "One Misty Moisty Morning"; and "Winter Song" by Jane Yolen (Yolen 1993b) are good starters. Children enjoy the bouncy rhythm created by alliteration and often memorize words quickly.

- Have students explore books of poetry to find their own examples of alliteration or onomatopoeia. They can add the poems they find to their personal anthologies, share them aloud, and copy them onto chart paper to be posted.

- Write some phrases using alliteration. Keep them simple at first by offering a noun and asking for two words to describe it. For example, "snow" could become "messy, mushy snow," and "ice" could become "frosty, freezing ice." Post the phrases you create together. Some students may want to expand the phrases into poems.

- Introduce tongue twisters as another way to play with language. *Fast Freddie Frog* by Ennis Rees (1993) is a good resource, but students will want to contribute their own. Not all tongue twisters are poems, but they do draw attention to alliteration and how we use language for special effects.

Play with Poetry Forms

Students need to experience enjoying poetry before they begin to look at the technical aspects of poetry forms. Children often become so caught up in the rules and regulations that they lose the pulse and emotion of what they want to say. Meaningful poetry must touch us personally. It dies when that element is missing.

Teaching About Poetry Forms

Ginnie: When I first started teaching poetry, I thought I had to teach students the rules for poetic forms. I would give them a recipe and help them work to meet the requirements of a form. Students counted syllables and tapped out the beat of iambic feet to satisfy rules. Sometimes they would sacrifice meaning to make their words fit a recipe or to make lines rhyme. Now I find that students don't need recipes, gimmicks, or prescriptions. When they are exposed to lots of poetry, they absorb its forms along with the meanings they want to express.

Now I show students some of the things poets do when they create poems. For example, some poets use lists, as Georgia Heard does in "Whale Chant" (Heard 1992). Others use a conversation between two people, as Nancy Springer does in "Talking to the Horse Trainer" (Springer 1994). Poets also use letters in poems, such as "Poem on My Pillow" by Brod Bagert (Goldstein 1992); "Thank You Stormy" by Nancy Springer (Springer 1994); and "In Response to Executive Order 9066" by Dwight Okita (Panzer 1994). I encourage students to try out some of these ideas in their own work.

Limericks are a form of light verse that follow a definite pattern of five lines: the first, second, and fifth lines consist of three feet and rhyme; and the third and fourth lines consist of two feet and rhyme. Edward Lear varies the pattern by using four lines, but the third line could easily be broken into two parts. For example:

> There was an old Person of Burton,
> Whose answers were rather uncertain;
> When they said, 'How d'ye do?' he replied, 'Who are you?'
> That distressing old person of Burton.

> —Edward Lear (Jackson 1951, 55)

Many editions of limericks are illustrated in full color, such as *Talkaty Talker* by Molly Manley (1994). One of her limericks is just right for the classroom:

> A remarkable guy from downtown,
> Known for reading his books upside down,
> Chose to stand on his head
> In his bed while he read
> And developed a permanent frown.

One of my colleagues, a teacher of the gifted and talented, teaches poetry forms to fifth graders as part of a lesson on contour line drawing to show a relationship between functional objects and poem outlines. Students choose an object in the classroom, such as a stapler, vase, or globe, then make a pencil sketch of it and talk about its functions. Then Susan describes the following elements of haiku, cinquain, and diamante.

A haiku, in its purest form, is an arrangement of sounds or syllables to form a 5-7-5 pattern on paper. Used in looser terms, it is three short, unrhymed lines, with the middle line longer than the other two. Usually, the theme of a haiku poem is the natural world, but there is often mention of human emotions or activity.

A cinquain is a stanza of five unrhymed lines. The lines progress from two, to four, to six, to eight syllables (or one, to two, to three, to four words); then the stanza ends with a two-syllable (or one-word) line. Each line has its own descriptor. The first line is a noun—the title of the poem. The second line has two words to describe the title; the third line contains three action words; the fourth line has four "feeling" or "emotion" words; and the last line is a synonym for the title. In a syllable cinquain, increase the number of syllables in each line.

A diamante is a diamond-shaped verse. The poem begins with one word, then grows word by word, line by line, until it tapers off again to end with one word.

When Susan's students write a poem about their sketch of the classroom object, they choose words that fit the guidelines for one of the above forms. As they select specific words to describe both form and function they also learn about the power of adjectives. Here are samples of students' diamantes:

Forms of Poetry

Narrative poem: Tells a story

Lyric poetry: States a mood or feeling

Limerick: Light verse, with an *aabba* / 1-2-5 and 3-4 rhyme scheme

Free Verse: Unrhymed verse, with an irregular metrical pattern

Concrete poetry: Words placed in the shape of the poem's subject

Haiku: Three lines, totaling seventeen syllables in a 5-7-5 pattern

Cinquain: Five unrhymed lines with 2, 4, 6, 8, and 2 syllables

Ballad: A story in verse meant to be sung

Stapler
Curved, movable
Toiling, working, buckling
Linking almost anything together
Hooking, clasping, connecting, joining
Holding tight metal
Shiny, black
Fastener

—Maggie

Telephone
Evolutionary, indescribable
Ringing, rotating, dialing
Highly advanced technology break-through
Puzzling, efficient, flexible
Effective, interesting
Communicator

—Nicolas

When students see that poets use many different forms—and create new forms—to express their ideas, they recognize the pliability of poetry. They are more willing to experiment when they write.

Helping Students Learn About Poetry Forms

- Show students guidelines for specific poetic forms through example and modeling. Choose a form to try out as a group. Urge students to experiment with one that suits their purpose.

- Find samples in which poets use various forms. Discuss how forms fit the message or echo the sense/meaning of the poem.

- Introduce specific forms, such as haiku, cinquain, diamante, and limerick. Make the forms available for elective assignments. Some students like the challenge of following a clear-cut form and counting syllables, so give them the guidelines.

- Introduce students who want to write rhymed verse to Marvin Terban's rhyming dictionary, *Time to Rhyme* (1994). Terban suggests different ways to use his dictionary for writing songs, verses, greeting cards, ads, or other things that rhyme. He gives examples of verses in which the ends of lines 1 and 2 rhyme with each other, lines 4, 5, and 6 rhyme with another sound, and lines 3 and 7 rhyme with still another sound, such as Samuel Patrick Smith's patriotic song, "America." The dictionary contains a wealth of information that is easily available for young students to use.

STRATEGY 11
The Poetry in Prose

Reading-writing workshop is a natural place to use poetry. Not only is poetry excellent material for reading, but it also serves as an excellent model for writing. Students discover that poetry is created from ordinary words used in uncommon ways, not from "poetic" or "fancy" language, which is sometimes hollow or vague. Such words do not make good poetry.

Poetry comes in sturdy language: it may hide in things people say, in headlines, or in sports announcements. With your students, watch for "found poetry"—words that resonate with unusual meaning. Marilyn helps students become aware of interesting language no matter where they find it, encouraging them to keep their eyes and ears open for possibilities in ordinary language. She often reminds them to watch for poetry in novels they read.

We do not want to set poetry behind a fence of formality; we want children to "mess around with it," to play with its forms, to manipulate its meanings, to see that meaning is uppermost. Students who find poetry in prose and who turn poems into prose learn that meaning is uppermost and that language is a plaything. Line breaks, punctuation, and the way poems are set on the page call attention to meaning. Students learn that poets manipulate the way poetry looks in order to manipulate what it means. Georgia Heard (1989) says,

> The concept of white space is similar to that of line breaks. Any time you see space in a poem, it means silence. Poets may use white space to make a break in the information or thought of a stanza; to slow the poem down; to encourage the reader to stop and reflect after a thought; to make the poem look more orderly; to set off the poem's final line and give it more impact; or to single out a line by surrounding it in silence. In the course of the workshop I introduce each of these uses of white space, one at a time. (63–64)

We can use Georgia Heard's ideas about white space to good effect; it gives students control over an important aspect of poetry.

Marilyn: Students have a lot more practice reading prose than they do reading poetry. They read prose narratives, biographies, textbooks, reports, and journal entries, but, due to their limited exposure, the poetry

Finding Poetry in Prose

they read may seem set off as separate and distinct. In a fifth-grade classroom, the teacher and I ask the students to find a passage of beautiful language as part of their personal response to prose. The choices they make reveal something about their interests, and the act of searching, choosing, copying, and reading a selection to classmates helps them build an inner sensitivity to the rhythms of language. They feel the poetry in prose.

Students who experience the links between poetry and prose feel comfortable reading and writing poetry; the connection removes the fence of formality. It helps students see that we can break rules, use no capitals, indent where it suits our purpose, or change the shape and structure of written language to bring about a particular effect for our reader. It shows that language is something we can play with—or change around to suit our fancy.

We encourage students to be on the lookout for beautiful language, wherever they see it. When they are reading *The Black Pearl* by Scott O'Dell (1967), we ask them to choose passages of language they think are beautiful. We write some of their choices on overhead transparencies and project them onto a screen so everyone can look at the same thing. Then we take turns reading. As the students read, I introduce the idea of line breaks as a signal to pause for meaning or as a way to slow the reader down. We experiment with line breaks by putting them in different places. I prefer to allow students to make awkward line breaks in the beginning rather than to present them with a right or wrong approach. When students read an awkward division or hear others read their prose poem, they often self-edit. Students are intrigued with the idea that they control decisions about what their reader does. This is Lauren's example, taken from *The Black Pearl* (68):

> At that moment
> A ray of light fell
> Through a window
> Full upon
> The Madonna.
> It shone upon the pearl
> She held in her hand
> And set it aglow
> And as I gazed at the pearl
> I began to wonder—
> For the first time
> Why such a
> Magnificent gift
> Had not protected my father
> Against the storm.

Charlie chooses this from page 40:

> It was round
> and smooth
> and the color of smoke.
> It filled my cupped hands.
> Then the sun's light struck
> deep into the thing
> and moved in silver
> swirls
> and I knew
> that it was not a rock
> that I held
> but a pearl
> the great pearl of heaven.

Jorge chooses this from page 32:

> The old man paddled slowly
> across the lagoon,
> carefully raising
> and
> lowering
> the paddle,
> as if he did not
> want to
> disturb the water.

Students realize that Scott O'Dell crafted words for *The Black Pearl* as carefully as a poet. We discuss how prose turned into poems becomes free verse.

After turning others' prose into poetry, students begin to look at their own prose for possibilities. One student, Peter, and I talk during writing workshop about baseball. Peter tells me that as a player you never know if you have made it safely to home plate while you are running. Here is what he wrote, starting with prose and moving to poetry.

Baseball

> When I hit the ball,
> on a hot summer day
> it makes me feel great,
> and running around the bases
> makes me feel free,
> free as a bird.

When I'm running to home
not knowing if I'm going to slide
or just cross the plate
and my teammates come,
come and slap me five
I know I hit a home run.

—Peter

Helping Students
Find Poetry
in Prose

Questions to Ask About
Line Breaks

Ask students:

Where do you want the reader to
pause?

Where do you want to keep the
reader in suspense?

Do you want readers to know this
quickly or do you want to make
them wait? Do you want to hold
them in suspense a while?

- Read aloud sentences that sound like poetry from Jane Yolen's *Owl Moon* (1987). For example, "Our feet crunched over the crisp snow and little gray footprints followed us. Pa made a long shadow, but mine was short and round. I had to run after him every now and then to keep up, and my short, round shadow bumped after me"(4). Also read aloud from Cynthia Rylant's *A Couple of Kooks* (1990): "Esther dear, time is fleeting. Will you, on your death bed, mourn the life you never cared to savor because you were too busy counting your losses?" (34). Read from Byrd Baylor's *I'm in Charge of Celebrations* (1986), or Cynthia Rylant's *When I Was Young in the Mountains* (1982). Discuss phrases that sound like poetry. Model for students your sensitivity to beautiful language; let them see how you take pleasure in its sounds. Read it again slowly.

- Ask students to watch for passages of beautiful language, record the nuggets, and read them to each other.

- Display samples of the beautiful language or vivid images they find on a word wall or a bulletin board.

- Ask students to record examples of rhythmic language in their notebooks or journals. Shelley Harwayne's students keep their examples in small spiral notebooks. They explain "This is where I keep words I might want to use in my own writing someday" (Harwayne 1992).

- Display prose passages from books and student writings. Ask students to suggest line breaks.

- Ask students to read the newspaper for "Found Poetry"—interesting tidbits of language. Look for items that stimulate a story. Write or tell it as a story, condense it to a poem and throw away the extra words.

STRATEGY 12
Poems in Personal Narrative

Personal narrative and memoirs contain the essence of good poetry—specific details and rich textures of emotionally-laden topics. Personal narrative becomes a wellspring for poetry; it draws upon meaningful subjects that are well known and important to the writer, and often are emotionally charged. Such topics lead to good poetry.

Ginnie: In a mini-lesson on personal narratives, I read several examples from Jean Little's *Hey, World, Here I Am!* (1989) and Sandra Cisneros's "Eleven" (1991). Students talk about the way authors reveal their personal lives in their writing, and then look at paragraphs they have written about themselves. David shows me an entry in his journal about his mother bugging him to clean up his room. It is a piece I have not seen before. "My mom keeps yelling at me to clean my room, especially the closet. Every day she says, 'David, clean your room. There are clothes all over the floor.' But I never do. I don't pay any attention to her. I just go out to play with my friends. One day, I will do it—just to shut her up." He tries rewriting the same ideas, and after several different attempts, he calls it "Cleaning My Closet":

> My closet is a mess.
> There's clothes all over the ground.
> Everyday I tell myself that I'm going to clean it,
> But I never do!
>
> When I finally do,
> It sparkles like sunshine.
> I say I'm going to keep it like that,
> But I never do!
>
> My mom gets upset.
> And yells at me constantly.
> She tells me to cleanup my closet & fold my clothes,
> But I never do!
>
> My closet is a mess.
> There's clothes all over the ground.

Moving from Personal Narrative to Poetry

Everyday I tell myself I'm going to clean it,
And I finally did!

And it's like that today!

—David

I use David's piece to talk about repetition in poetry, pointing out that repetition underscores important ideas and establishes a rhythm. The students decide that repetition makes readers comfortable by giving them a familiar phrase.

Helping Students Convert Personal Narrative to Poetry

- Have students work in pairs or individually to turn prose into poems. Share them with the class.

- Have students find or write a poem to accompany a report. This helps them to discover that poetry can express the strong emotions surrounding controversial topics, such as preserving the rain forests, hunting whales, and homelessness.

- Have students work in pairs to write poems in two voices. Each voice represents a side of a debate about a controversial issue, or one voice acts as prey and one as predator.

- Combine both poetry and prose in a story poem.

S T R A T E G Y   1 3
Think Like a Poet

Poets look beyond surfaces to find the essence of objects or experiences. To look at anything the way a poet does is to observe it closely. When students are immersed in poetry, they inevitably begin to write their own. Frequently the poetry they write sounds like the poetry they read. This is not cause for alarm because most writers imitate or try on for size the style of other writers they admire. They say, "I tried to write like Poe when I was reading Poe and like Hemingway when I was reading Hemingway. I tried on other people's styles in the process of developing my own." Teachers who read aloud good literature give developing writers good models. Reading aloud, especially from poetry, is one of the most powerful tools we have for teaching writing.

Ginnie: As my classes begin to enjoy and save poems that they love, we discover that we can turn to poetry for information. When we study the Native American cultures, for example, we find that nothing better expresses the anguish of displacement and loss than the poetry of the Native Americans themselves. After students read many such poems, they begin to compose their own. As I recognize the empathy and pathos within their compositions, I know they understand that period of our history very well. Weaker students, particularly, benefit from this exposure to another genre for information. The vivid images, repetitions, and rhythms help them to remember new ideas and concepts.

Sometimes I find that poetry draws students beyond their initial reactions to things. In a science unit, for instance, the fifth graders are "grossed out" by the idea of dissecting sterilized owl pellets to discover the number of prey animals it takes to feed an owl family. The thought of investigating meal worms brings the same shudder response. The students need information that will override their gut feelings of repulsion. To combat these feelings, I share poems and books that express the wonder of these new worlds. For example, *Owl Lake* (Tejima 1987) uses a brief poetic text and dramatic woodcuts to tell the drama of an owl's nocturnal search for food. Ruth Heller's *Chickens Aren't the Only Ones* (1981) speaks of the miracle of an egg's potential throughout the animal kingdom. Poems can keep us open to new experiences, reveal complex truths, and expose us to beauty in the least expected of places.

- Use poetry to make some observations about a subject. For example, read "Lobster" in Joy N. Hulme's *What If?* (1993, 19).

> He's upside down and inside out;
> He's backwards and he's sideways.
> His bones are out; his skin is in;
> He lives in ocean tideways.
>
> He walks on hairy, spindly legs
> That smell and breathe and hear,
> And scurries backward in retreat
> Whenever danger's near.
>
> His jaws chew sideways, but his teeth
> Are found inside his tummy;
> And while he gobbles fishy fare,
> His feet taste if it's yummy.
>
> His kidneys hide inside his head;
> His brain's beside his throat;

> And when it gets too small for him,
> He sheds his bony coat.
>
> He has one claw to clobber with;
> The other cuts and saws;
> And when he frolics on the beach,
> He plays with SANDY CLAWS.

Have students pick out the characteristics and habits of a lobster from the verses. Discuss how Joy Hulme plays with the facts to make them humorous. Ask them what else they would like to know about lobsters, and then refer them to other books and resources for answers. Use the new information to create your own verses or stories.

- Collect poems about families around the world. Compare the tone as well as the content. Help your students to notice similarities and differences in families everywhere by asking them questions as you share the poetry with them. Lead them to make universal connections and to seek additional information as they read trade books, memoirs, and histories. You may find that when they begin to tell the stories of their own families, they will try poetry, too.

- Use poems as models for writing. The third graders use Mary Ann Hoberman's *A House Is a House for Me* (1978) as a model for writing about animals they are reading about. Here are some examples of their work:

> A mother is a house for a baby.
>
> A mailbox is a house for mail.
>
> A book is a house for a story.

As students read about coyotes in the desert, crabs along the shore, or eagles on cliffs, ask them to write their own verses to the same cadence and rhyme scheme. Have them use *Winter Barn* by Peter Parnall (1986) and *Cactus Hotel* by Brenda Guiberson (1991) as models. In the following poem, poet Brod Bagert describes the effects of models in "First Steps."

> Young poets imitate.
> Mature poets steal.
>
> —T. S. Eliot

> I read my first poem
> And I felt like frowning;

It sounded too much
Like Elizabeth Browning.

Then in my next poem
I noticed a change,
I was Emily Dickinson—
Quiet and strange.

Now it's happened again,
Please don't think I'm weird,
But today I'm Walt Whitman,
Without the long beard.

When I read all my writing
I discover a rule:
I write like whomever
We're reading at school.

> —Brod Bagert (Cullinan and Galda 1994, 387)

- Discuss fragile ecosystems, extinction, global pollution, or destroying the rain forests, and then expand understanding through poetry. Read "The Galapagos Tortoise" in Georgia Heard's *Creatures of Earth, Sea, and Sky* (1992, 31). Also read the following poem from her book:

Will We Ever See?

Will we ever see a tiger again,
stalking its prey with shining eyes?

Will we see the giant orangutan
inspecting its mate for fleas?

Or a California condor
feeding on the side of a hill?

Or a whooping crane
walking softly through a salty marsh?

Or hear the last of the blue whales
singing its sad song under the deep water?

- Use a variety of poems about a topic—humorous, lyrical, free verse, short, and long. Use poems by Eve Merriam in *Fresh Paint* (1986), Langston Hughes in *The Dream Keeper and Other Poems* (1986), and Eloise Greenfield in *Honey, I Love* (1978).

- Take students to the library to search for poems that give information and provide a point of view.

- Use poems more than once. Introduce two or three new poems about a topic each day but loop back over familiar poems, too. Ask students to select ones they remember and like best. Reread the poems from earlier sessions. Students begin to memorize the poems they like; they build a storehouse of poetry that lasts a lifetime.

- Add favorite poems to the class anthology or individual student anthologies. Post copies of the poems around the classroom to enjoy any time of day.

STRATEGY 14

Notice Connections and Make Popcorn

Ideas become the images children store in the museums of their minds. Vivid images are the primary substance or essence of poetry. Words can create such clear pictures in our mind's eye that they stay with us always— we only need to close our eyes to recall a vision words caused us to create. Imaging, the ability to imagine, is a valuable thought process. Poetry, packed with images, helps us to see beyond the literal world.

Jean Little, noted author, describes a childhood memory in her autobiography, *Little by Little* (1987). One morning her mother woke her up very early for a dreaded doctor's appointment by bringing her a plate with an orange cut into sections, each with its skin on. Jean pretended the orange segments were sailboats and lined them up, one behind the other, with their orange sails bright against a dark windowsill. The glowing orange sailboats looked so beautiful that Jean could hardly bear to spoil them by eating one, and she realized with a pang that in a week, even in a day, perhaps, she would forget how beautiful they looked. She vowed to remember the orange sailboats as long as she lived. Recalling this moment in her autobiography, she says, "What mattered was that for the first time I saw my world and my life as something that belonged to me, and began to put small scraps of time away in a place where I could take them out and look at them whenever I needed to remember" (93).

Jean Little made a connection between a seemingly insignificant event in her life and what seemed important enough to write about in her journal; she realized that tidbits from her own life were worthwhile writing topics. Students, too, can make connections between their lives and the poetry they read and write. They learn to treasure small events in daily life—

to see them as meaningful topics worthy of writing about in poems or prose. Recognizing the literary value of simple life events makes it easier for writers to choose topics, to explore a variety of possible writing projects, and to savor their lives. It also helps them to discover that revising drafts, setting unfinished work aside, going back to drafts, or throwing them away is acceptable behavior for all writers, especially poets.

Marilyn: If I want students to be eager to write poetry, I start writers workshop by reading poetry. I choose poems that spark interest, have a variety of moods, and show a variety of styles. I realize that by continually reading poetry and by building classroom collections and personal anthologies, we are building students' repertoire of poetry topics and forms.

Making Connections and Choosing a Topic

When I surround students with poetry they like, they automatically start to write poetry. Finding a poem topic is no different from searching for a prose topic, and when students hear and read lots of poetry, they see that many simple events are worthwhile writing topics.

When students read a lot of poetry, they are not only simply enjoying it but they are also making connections with events, places, and people in their own lives. Together we flip through a book of poetry to see the variety of topics that poets treat. As we skim *A Jar of Tiny Stars* (Cullinan 1995), we see topics ranging from climbing trees, a kitten, John F. Kennedy, Martin Luther King, windshield wipers, and Daddy fixing breakfast to pebbles, recess, and winter clothes. Several topics emerge from this type of browsing. When we are through, I model making a topic choice by thinking aloud. I explain that if I sat down to write right now, I would probably write about pebbles because pebbles carry special meaning for me. Here is the story I tell.

> When we vacation in Northern Michigan, my family can be found, heads down at the water's edge, looking for Petosky stones. Petosky stones are rather plain when dry, but with a coat of water they are magnificent. With an intricate five-sided design, they are reminders of coral in an ancient saltwater sea. Somewhere we heard the legend that if you find a stone with a ring entirely around it, it brings you good luck. I've not always had good luck but, like a poem, the pleasure of the legend and a stone with a perfect line is pleasure enough.

Students see that a topic that succeeds as a poem often has personal meaning and feelings and can start with "prose" thoughts.

When we discuss possible topics and read sample poems, some students quickly grasp the idea of personal meaning and begin to write. In Figure 3, one student, Mary, talks about the special relationship she had with her grandmother.

Other students begin to write immediately because they have made a connection between simple objects, such as pebbles or marbles, and thoughts about life (see Figure 4).

While the students who find their topic quickly begin to write, I am free to conference with students who feel they have nothing about which to write. That feeling always disappears once we talk and uncover a "hot" topic—that they love sports or are experienced in karate. The two poems by Tommy and Luke are by reluctant poets—boys who initially feel they have nothing important to say.

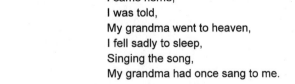

My Grandma And Me
MARY

I Was Born,
My grandma was proud,
My first birthday,
My grandma laughed and she cried,
I met Junior the dog,
My grandma snapped photos,
I walked,
My grandma watched in delight,
I sniffled,
My grandma sang softly
I grew,
My Grandma's heart grew
I got pneumonia,
My grandma got cancer
I got better,
My grandma got better
I went to school,
My grandma slept in a hospital bed with machines all
around her,
And then one day while I was in school,
I got a headache and then a stomache,
My grandma had died,
I came home,
I was told,
My grandma went to heaven,
I fell sadly to sleep,
Singing the song,
My grandma had once sang to me.

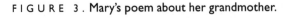

F I G U R E 3 . Mary's poem about her grandmother.

Marbles
Lauren

Sometimes I think
        that the world is like marbles,
                Because you can arrange them
And re-arrange them from time to time
        Like the future
                And the past.
But along the way, they may get
        smudged with fingerprints
                or chipped
So you have to
        polish them
                on your good Sunday shirt.
And after that, you can look
        at your collection
and hold them up to the light
        and notice
that each one is different
                in size
                        or color
And each one is yours.
And then, when you put
        your marbles back
                in your velvet pouch
                        and they
                                click together
It's like the world
        is turning
                in the palm
                        of your hand
And everything
        is as un-perfect
                as it ought to be.

FIGURE 4. Lauren's poem about marbles.

Tommy writes four lines with the idea that sports are fun, upsetting, hilarious, and heartbreaking. In the first revision he explains what each word means by adding four more lines, and then, in his last revision, he sums up the poem with a final sentence:

Sports

Sports are fun
When you hit a home run
Sports are upsetting
When you lose
Sports are hilarious
When you make a stupid play
Sports are heartbreaking
When you lose the Championship game

Sports are like "LIFE."

Luke tells me about his karate experiences; while he talks, his conversation has a staccato effect that shows up in the poem.

Karate

"bow"
　　　"fighting stance"
"fight"
　　lunging backfist
　　　　reverse hook kick
inverted round kick
　　"break"
　　　　"point"
"fight"
　　side kick
　　　　front kick
round kick
　　"break"
　　　　"return to the ring"
"fight"
　　　　front punch
　　back punch
　　　　round kick
"break"
　　"winner."

Luke discovers a form that enhances his topic.

The popcorn image in the strategy title comes from poet Arnold Adoff's (1988) description of his false starts in writing and rewriting. One day, he recalls, visiting students called him the "popcorn poet." As they watched him toss balls of crumpled paper into his wastebasket, the wadded up rejected pages reminded them of popcorn balls.

Hearing this description makes us feel more comfortable about our own crumpled pages on the floor; we savor Adoff's delicious, vivid image. When we struggle to express ideas, write, abandon drafts, rewrite, throw away, expand, and discard—we too are making popcorn.

. . . .

Helping Students Make Topic Choices and Explore Rewriting

- Expose students to a variety of topics. Read poems or just titles and a few lines to give an overview of the array.

- Conference with children having difficulty getting started. Ask them about their interests, projects they are working on, and after-school activities. As they talk, have them keep a list of possible things they could write about. When they articulate an idea, encourage them to shift from thought to paper. Some children write eloquently about writer's block.

- Ask students to share some of their beginning ideas before the session ends. As they share, they receive positive reinforcement from peers for their choice of words, vivid images, and connections. They discover from their listeners where they might clarify or expand an idea. Frequent sharing of works in progress helps all the writers in the room.

- Keep a list of your students' topics, works in progress, and finished poems. It helps you to know which students need help finding a topic, who needs a conference, or perhaps who is not using the writing time wisely. This helps in planning and keeps the class on task. Also set a date for work to be finished and shared.

- Be patient with students. They write lots of poems of questionable quality before they produce a gem. Help them reach for the next level in their writing. Read aloud poems from Sara Holbrook's *Nothing's the End of the World* (1995) to show how a poet captures the pre-teenager's voice of complaint. When students hear others' problems described in verse, they will want to express their own "end of the world."

- Help student authors examine the effects of the language they use in poems. Are the words active and alive? Where can they substitute a word to make the meaning clear, to accentuate the author's voice, or to give the poem more energy? Encourage them to use the thesaurus and to experiment with metaphor and simile.

- Show students that punctuation serves a purpose in poetry. Copy some poems from Kimberly Colen's *Peas and Honey: Recipes for Kids (With a Pinch of Poetry)* (1995) onto overhead transparancies or charts. Read the poems aloud with and without the punctuation to illustrate how changes in punctuation affect meaning and sound. Remind students that if they want their poems to rush and run along, they may not need any punctuation at all. Students actually feel exuberant about their choice to eliminate conventions of written language in writing poetry; they delight in freedom from rules.

....

PART THREE

Using Poetry in Content Areas

Educational practice is changing rapidly in response to research by cognitive psychologists that clearly shows how people learn and how the mind works. Studies show that we make connections between things we already know and new material we are learning (Just and Carpenter 1980; Rumelhart and McClelland 1980). Furthermore, we learn best when we have a schema—a framework around which to organize the new material (Anderson 1978; Anderson, Pichert, and Shirey 1979). In one study, a team of researchers at the Center for the Study of Reading gave one group of participants a list of thirty items to pick up at the grocery store (Anderson, Spiro, and Anderson 1978). They were given two minutes to study the list, and then were asked to write down what they remembered. Most remembered only six or eight items. The researchers gave another group the same list of thirty items, again with two minutes to study the list before they wrote the items down. This time they told the participants, "You're having a dinner party tonight. You'll have an appetizer, a salad, a main course, dessert and coffee. This is what you need to get at the grocery store." Most of this group remembered twenty-six or twenty-eight items because they had a framework—a schema. They remembered more because they had organized categories to cluster items around.

Schema theory research shows that our minds work best by creating little webs of understanding; we hook one thing onto another to create a schema, a semantic web of meaning. Knowing how children learn brings changes in the school curriculum.

We used to teach a "cha cha cha" curriculum where we "cha cha cha'ed" from one subject to another: we taught forty-five minutes of math—cha cha cha—forty-five minutes of social studies—cha cha cha—forty-five minutes of science. We jumped from one subject to another so that we could "get everything in." Today we know that learners don't shift gears that quickly. Now we integrate the curriculum into larger chunks of meaning and allot bigger blocks of time for integrated studies.

In today's curriculum we help students make connections by integrating subject areas in logical ways. Instead of teaching curriculum areas as separate subjects, we organize them around unifying themes, people, universal ideas, organizational plans. One particular unifying thread has been the literature we use across the curriculum. In a literature-based program, we use a variety of genres (picture books, fiction, informational books, poetry) as well as a variety of formats (video, computers, CDs, books, newspapers, magazines) to explore a subject. Students learn in different ways; this includes something to appeal to every learning style.

Poetry is an amazingly effective, but underused, genre in literature-based curricula. Poetry appeals to all types of students—the reluctant reader, the child with special needs, the gifted and talented student, the average child. Because poetry usually has only a few words on a line, it looks manageable to the hesitant reader. Its brevity makes it appealing and it taps the essence of a subject, presenting that essence in brief, crystallized statements.

Poetry does more, is more, and gives more than other types of literature. Poetry presents more than dry facts—and often does so in a humorous way. It also provides sensory experiences that modern children need. Some children grow up in environments where they seldom have a chance to feel the smooth, slimy touch of mud; the rough-textured bark of a tree; the crumbling, gritty grains of sand. Poetry recreates vivid sensory experiences; its words give children the sense of touching, feeling, smelling, and seeing. Once you use it, poetry is a genre that becomes a staple in your curriculum.

Science, Social Studies, and Math

Science

The primary function of reading and writing poetry is for enjoyment—not to learn or teach facts. In some cases, however, poems can help make a topic memorable because they use highly charged words and help to create vivid images. Poetry reinforces concepts students should remember. The following strategies make science facts memorable: Enrich Science with Poetry; Webbing Science and Poetry; Science Research Reports and Writing Poetry; Think Like a Scientist; Science Sentence Poems; Science Riddles; and Science Biographies.

STRATEGY 15
Enrich Science with Poetry

When I talk to teachers they tell me "Give us poetry to wrap around what we have to do, to integrate it into every area of the curriculum. We don't have time to treat it separately, but we can weave it into what we already do." Poetry fits well with science because both require close observation.

Ginnie: On his way home from the vet one day, my son brings his seven-foot, pet red-tailed boa constrictor, Dude, to my classroom for a visit. I use the opportunity to open students' eyes to the ways poems enrich an experience. After the visit, we create a bulletin board with photographs of Dude and search for poetry about snakes to celebrate our introduction to this unusual pet. I am astounded by the number of poems we find—in all styles and voices. Some are funny, such as Shel Silverstein's "I'm Being Swallowed by a Boa Constrictor" (Silverstein 1974), and "The Snake" by Jack Prelutsky (Prelutsky 1983). Others give information, such as "Dressing Like a Snake" (Heard 1992). One, May Swenson's "Redundant Journey" (Swenson 1993), is written from a snake's point of view. The snapshots and poems invite students to find out more about snakes. I pile a stack of books about snakes conveniently on the table below the bulletin board.

Going to School with Dude the Snake

Enriching Science Studies with Poems

- Use a science activity, an unusual plant, incubating eggs, a fish tank, or a collection of rocks and minerals as the topic for a bulletin board. Locate poems that express feelings about and ones that give information on the topic. Mix poems with informational paragraphs and photographs in the display.

- Invite students to add poems to the bulletin board.

- Copy poems in print large enough to be seen from a distance. When poetry is visible, children read it aloud and share it often. Reluctant readers join in because they find shared reading very comfortable.

- Spark color and interest in the bulletin board by adding photographs, drawings, cutouts, and realia. Dude's most recently shed skin frames our posters.

- Place informational books, picture books, and fiction about the subject close to the bulletin board. Select from many reading levels, so that all students can participate.

- Create poetry posters for the bulletin board. Use students' writing and that of favorite poets.

- Read Julie Brinckloe's book *Fireflies* (1985) when you study fireflies, and read the riddle "Firefly" by Elizabeth Maddox Roberts, in William Jay Smith and Carol Ra's *Behind the King's Kitchen* (1992, 25).

- Read Randall Jarrell's fantasy, *The Bat Poet* (1967), Janell Cannon's picture book, *Stellaluna* (1993), and Georgia Heard's "Bat Patrol" in *Creatures of Earth, Sea, and Sky* (1992) when you study bats.

STRATEGY 16
Webbing Science and Poetry

A spider's web is an intricate network of fine threads woven into a pattern used to catch insects. A semantic web is a visual display of information used to show connections among facts, ideas, and categories. Teachers use webbing to plan thematic units, to develop background knowledge, to record brainstorming, to organize responses, and to do a variety of other things. Students use webbing to present information, to organize what they know and want to learn about a subject, and to do a number of other things. For example, if we were to web a topic such as "weather," we would put that word in a circle in the center of a page and then list types of weather in smaller circles around the central one. The outer circles might contain words such as *storms, rain, fog, sunshine,* and *clouds.* The circles that would branch off from "storms" might include *hurricanes, thunderstorms,* and *tropical storms.* Words such as *lightning, thunder,* and *rain* might branch off from "thunderstorms" (see Figure 5). At any point, we could incorporate poems into webs to illustrate concepts.

Webbing Science
Topics and Poems

Ginnie: This year I'm a science teacher in a departmentalized sixth grade. On the first day of school I stack a large pile of poetry books on the table at the front of the classroom. I tell each group that our first unit of study will be "The Blue Planet" and ask them what they think that might

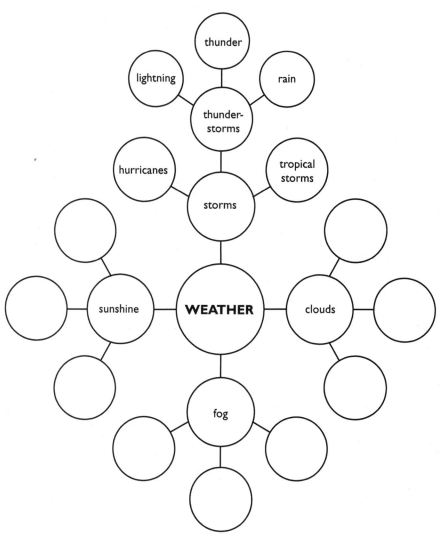

FIGURE 5. A weather web.

mean. Without giving any hints, I encourage them to discuss their ideas. Eventually, most agree that "The Blue Planet" must be Earth, because of all its water. I ask teams of two students to find a poem from the poetry collection that makes them think of "The Blue Planet" and then copy it onto a 3 × 5 inch card, along with the title and author. The students work enthusiastically to find and copy a poem. We attach loops of tape to the back of each poetry card and, after reading each poem aloud, post them randomly on a large chalkboard.

Later, we look at the assortment of poems and begin to search for connections among them. First, we group them into large categories under labels such as Weather, Plants, Land, Animals, Water, and Air. We pull cards from one spot and repost them in another until we have rows of cards under each heading (see Figure 6). Then we discuss how the categories relate to each other. As we draw arrows connecting one group of poems to another, it becomes apparent that every living thing on our earth depends on something else for its survival. Plants depend on water, air, sunlight, and soil. Animals depend on plants, other animals, water, and air. We note that sometimes these relationships are disturbed by acts of nature and by human acts. Our complex web shows the interdependence between earth's resources and organisms. We decide that there are still more arrows to draw before we are ready to begin our unit on Oceanography.

As we look back at our web, we see which areas need more information. Those areas become the focus for further reading and research. As students gather more information, we add it to the web, and we examine how the new data changes the relationships already shown. We note, for instance, that we did not consider the role of microbes, such as plankton and bacteria, when we created our web. As we read, however, we find that their

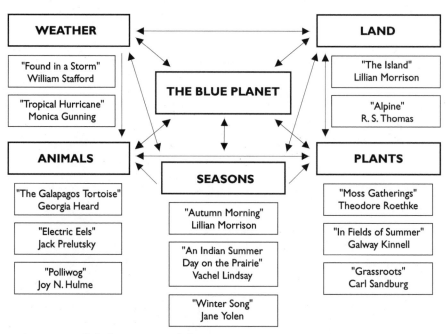

FIGURE 6. Relating poems and themes.

importance becomes evident, and our crisscrossing arrows become even more complex.

- Ask students to locate poems related to an area of study you are undertaking (e.g. mammals, a microscope, the world, space, the desert).

- Categorize the poems according to a plan that seems reasonable to the students and to you.

- Create a poetry web with the categories and poems. Locate areas in the web that need more information. Encourage students to generate questions to investigate during the study. List their questions on a chart to be displayed and referred to throughout the study.

- Ask students to write the answers to their questions first in prose, then to turn some of the information into poetry. (See Strategy 11 for techniques.)

- Prepare a K-W-L chart for a topic of study. List the information students *know* (collectively), what they *want* to find out, and what they have *learned* (as the study progresses). Collect poems to enrich the topic of study.

Webbing Science and Poetry with Your Students

STRATEGY 17
Science Research Reports and Writing Poetry

Painters speak to us through their art; poets speak to us through their words. Our lives are enriched by what they see and help us to see. They interpret the world we all share. When students compare informational writing and poetry, or art and photographs, they discover that people describe the world differently. They learn to see differently when they use different ways to describe the same topic themselves.

Marilyn: Our school science curriculum requires fourth graders to study the Long Island seashore—the rocky, north shore beaches and the sandy, south shore ones. Students take field trips to beaches on both shores.

Two Ways of Seeing

They kneel beside tide pools to cradle tiny crabs in their hands before releasing them back to the bay. They sit in the sand to draw pictures of the delicate yet strong plants, such as sea grass, that help to keep the beaches from eroding. For the culminating project of this unit, they write a research report on one aspect of the beaches—water, plants, animals, or shoreline.

I meet with the class during some of their writers workshop time. Their teacher and I discuss integrating poetry and decide this is the perfect time. I start one workshop with students seated comfortably on the floor around me. We read poetry from Georgia Heard's *Creatures of Earth, Sea, and Sky* (1992) and Pat Moon's *Earth Lines: Poems for the Green Age* (1991). I read the poems once; while the students sit silently immersed in the mood, I read them again. I watch the students' faces reflect understanding of the poets' concerns. We talk about the poems and the issues they raise. Students mention noticing repeated lines, but mostly they notice the setting of mood.

During our second workshop together, I read the poetry again. This time I take requests and show a few poems on the overhead projector. Using "The Galapagos Tortoise" and "Elephant Warning" (Heard 1992), we discuss the information that poets include and how the poems might look written as a paragraph or as notes for a report. We discuss the phrases that are repeated for emphasis. I mention casually that most of the poems do not rhyme and that poets must decide first what they want to say, and then how they want it to look (line breaks).

We ask students to skim their science reports to find five or so facts that they think are interesting and then to list them at the top of a page. We tell them to play around with these bits of information. Some feel the sense of poetry in their information immediately and begin to write. We encourage others to write in paragraph form first, just to get their ideas down. The other teacher and I hold conferences with students. Most important, we remember to *ask* not *tell*; when there is a question of meaning, we ask students what they were trying to say and if they can think of other ways to say it. We do not tell them how to fix their work or suggest ways that it could be better. We let the poem lead the conference. We ask for clarification and elaboration, and as students answer, their poems expand. Some are ready to discuss line breaks, so we read the lines to see how they sound. Sometimes I read their lines to them a few different ways. This helps them see possibilities and choose which they prefer, or maybe come up with another way. I sometimes read a draft and ask them to consider if there is another order of ideas that might read more fluently.

One student, Colleen, sits with a lovely poem that rhymes, but the last stanza seems forced. She is trying to keep the rhyme pattern but is sacrificing meaning for it. She has written, "In your cell you lay damp and curled/ appreciate your little world/ you may yet become a pearl/ you can hide beneath the swirl/ it may last a little while." I ask Colleen if that has been a hard part to rhyme; she admits it is. I ask if she can keep the idea but look at the words in the last sentence to see if she can rearrange them into a non-rhyming statement. This is the finished poem:

Hear Our Cry

Buzz of insects hear our cry
as salty ocean waves roll by,
Your environment so thick and wet,
may not be the best home yet.

Periwinkles hear our cry
when the tide is low
when the tide is high
as you cling on tall grass, remember,
this rest may be your last

Spit of fiddlers hear our cry
as your underground environment
soon is dry
In your cell you lay damp and curled
appreciate your little world

while it lasts

—Colleen

Another child, Kirk, begins with a list of facts about octopuses:

1. have no bones

2. hard to kill

3. look like giant spiders

4. can go without months of eating

Then he adds statements:

Octopuse are the giant spiders of the deep double cross them and you'll be gone bones and all with there hard beek they can wate for months but usally doesn't don't ever double cross one

Here is Kirk's second draft, written as a poem:

Octapusses are giant spiders
of the deep. Double cross one and

you'll be gone bones and all. He'll
chew you up with that parrots beek.
The one hard spot in there body.
So don't ever double cross one.

Here is his final draft:

The Giant Spiders of the Deep

Octopuses are the giant spiders of
the deep.

Double cross one and you'll be gone,
bones and all.

He'll chew you up with that parrot's
beak, the one hard spot in its body.

So don't double cross an Octopus.

—Kirk

Another student, Cathy, begins with a list of facts about seaweed (see
Figure 7). Then she expands her list into statements (see Figure 8).
Here is her next draft, written as a poem:

There are millions
of different kinds of seeweed

Ribbon like and delicate

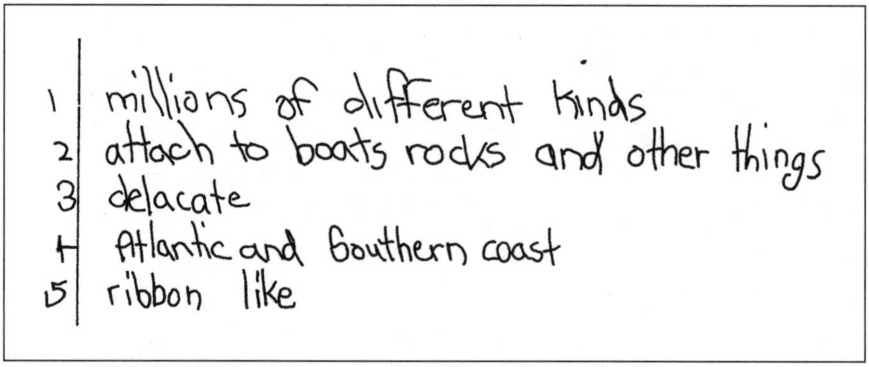

1 millions of different kinds
2 attach to boats rocks and other things
3 delacate
4 Atlantic and Southern coast
5 ribbon like

FIGURE 7. Cathy's facts about seaweed.

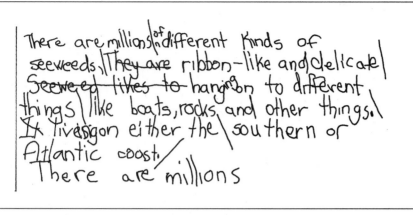

FIGURE 8. Cathy's statements about seaweed.

> Hanging on to different things
> like boats, rocks and other things
>
> Living on either the . . .

This is her final draft:

> There are millions
> Of different kinds of seaweed,
>
> Ribbon-like and delicate,
>
> Hanging on to different things
> Like boats, rocks and pinkish shells,
>
> Living on either
>
> The southern or Atlantic coasts.
>
> There are
> millions.
>
> —Cathy

Pat, another student, chooses horseshoe crabs. He also begins with a list of facts (see Figure 9). Figure 10 shows Pat's expanded statements. His final draft is written as a poem:

The Fossil of the Sea

> Horseshoe crabs
> have been around

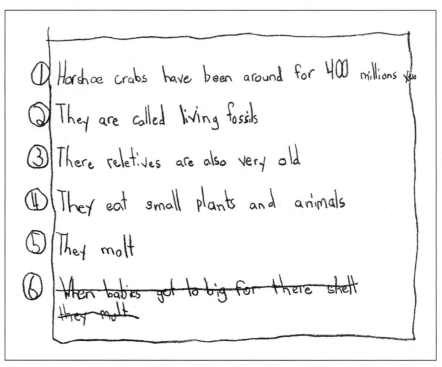

FIGURE 9. Pat's list of facts about horseshoe crabs.

for 400 million years,
because they haven't
been hunted for any part of their body.
They are called

LIVING FOSSILS

because they have been around since the

DINOS!!!

Their relatives, the
spider crabs,
have been around for so long,
because they haven't been
tampered with either.

—Pat

The students are able to move to poetry rather easily because they are so well versed in their topic. They have lots of information to include in

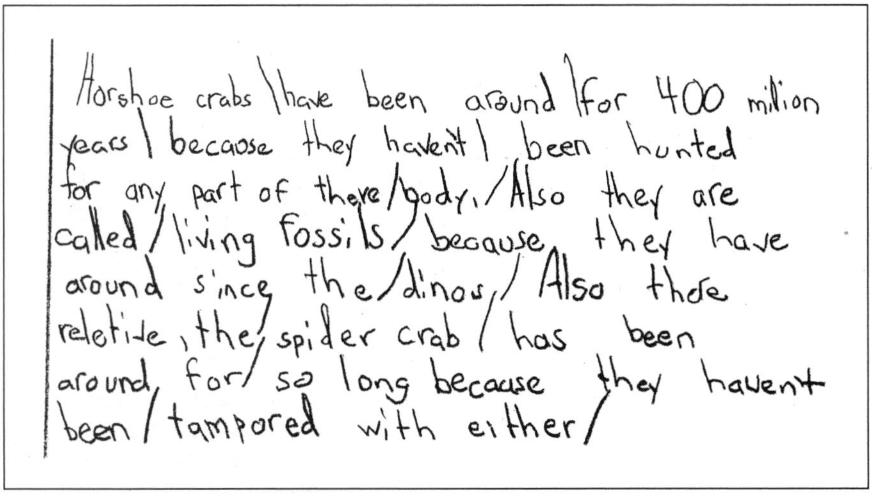

Horshoe crabs \have been around \for 400 million years \ because they haven't \ been hunted for any part of there\ body, /Also they are called / living fossils / because, they have around since the / dinos, / Also there reletive, the / spider crab / has been around, for / so long because they havent been / tampored with either /

FIGURE 10. Pat's statements about horseshoe crabs.

their poems. They enjoy their own poems as much as, if not more than, those of the published poets.

* Develop an anthology of poems you love to read and share them with students. Include as many curriculum-related topics as possible.

* Help students to reflect on their learning when they gather information on a science research topic. Encourage them to pull out points of interest and important aspects to discover the essence of a subject.

* Encourage students to write about their ideas in any form that projects their feelings about the topic.

* Conference with students to expose them to styles of poems, rhyming patterns, internal line rhyme, end rhyme, free verse, line breaks, stanzas, and list poems. Let the poem lead your conference while you explore ideas with the student.

* Show students different poem styles whether the examples are about the same topic or not. Even if the child is writing about spiders, a poem about rain might be a relevant example because of its style.

* Treasure the students' work. Publish it in class books or hold poetry readings for others. Invite other class groups and parents to celebrate with you.

Helping Students Explore Two Ways of Seeing

STRATEGY 18

Think Like a Scientist

Scientists observe with a clear eye, record their observations in precise, descriptive language, and craft their expressions. Poets do the same thing.

Making Bartholomew's Oobleck

Recipe for Oobleck

1 16-ounce box of cornstarch
$1\frac{1}{2}$ to $1\frac{2}{3}$ cups of water
5 drops of green food coloring

Oobleck flows like a liquid until sudden force is exerted on it, and then it behaves like a solid. You cannot "mix" this mixture. "Lift" the oobleck from the bottom to the top with your fingers to stir it. Let it sit 30 minutes, covered, before use. If the mixture seems too thin at first, let it sit uncovered and the extra water will evaporate. Oobleck dries out after students have worked with it so add water as needed. It can be used over and over if stored covered in the refrigerator. Note: Cover work areas for easy cleanup. Don't dump it down the sink—it will clog the drain!

(Cronemeyer 1993)

Ginnie: One day, I happen to see a recipe for "Oobleck" based on Dr. Seuss's book *Bartholomew and the Oobleck* (1949). One morning, well before school begins, I decide to try it with my science class. I prepare by mixing a box of cornstarch with some water and food coloring. Although I have read about the mixture, I am not prepared for what actually happens. I invite all of my colleagues who walk past my classroom to come in and "stir" it up for themselves; they are as shocked as I am. The surface of the mixture looks runny, as though it will easily pour and drip. But a spoon does not penetrate the surface without a push. When it does, the underneath layers crack apart, only to "melt" and fill in once the spoon is removed. It is fascinating stuff—fun for play and experiments. I can't wait to see what my students make of it.

We have just begun a study unit on matter: What it is, what it isn't, how it behaves. At the beginning of this day's session, we review what we already know and then discuss how scientists gain their knowledge about different forms of matter. As students break into groups, I encourage them to use their five senses to start exploring matter, but warn them first not to taste, touch, or smell unknown substances without teacher permission. Then I distribute cups of Oobleck to each group, along with a tray and a tongue depressor.

For the next ten minutes or so, students mold, pour, stir, chop, and mix this strange substance. Marcus takes a lump and holds it in his palm, elbow cocked and resting on the table. Slowly, the glob begins to move down his wrist. "Marcus," I ask, "Would you say that the Oobleck is dripping or running down your arm?"

"No," he says, "It's just *oozing* down real slowly."

John adds, "It travels when you try to pour it, but it falls apart when you try to chop it up. Then, it comes back together again when you leave it alone!"

Dorothy says, "When it gets on your hands, it dries up like powder. You can scrape the pieces back into the cup and they blend right in again."

I ask several other questions as I weave my way among the tables and encourage students to talk about their experiences with this unknown mass (mess!). Finally, they write together to describe Oobleck—what it looks like, what it will and will not do, how it feels, what surprises them. We use the language they generate to create list poems about Oobleck. (See Glossary for a definition of list poems.) I remind them that poetry begins with strong images and experiences, but the language of poetry must be vivid enough to carry the message to the next reader.

Helping Students Create List Poems from Their Discoveries

- Collect samples of poems containing lists; keep them available as models. Shel Silverstein's "Sarah Cynthia Sylvia Stout Would Not Take the Garbage Out" in his book *Where the Sidewalk Ends* (1974, 70–71) is a variation on the list poem form.

- Create list poems in a situation where you are exploring new language or concepts. See Georgia Heard's *Creatures of Earth, Sea, and Sky* (1992) for a list of whales in "Whale Chant." You can find poems that examine every nuance of water from a trickle to a roar. Ask students to contribute to a class list of words and phrases to describe an action or phenomenon. Shape a poem with the words and phrases. Move parts around until the words and verses flow easily. Encourage them to look for words that give the full picture without relying on "tired" language.

- Don't be concerned with beginnings or endings. List poems don't have to "go" anywhere. Instead, just enjoy playing with language. Encourage students to use it as precisely as possible and with as much color as they can. This requires full use of all the senses, so allow plenty of time for students to observe, listen, touch, taste, and smell.

- Ask students to work in groups of two or three to compose list poems. Share finished or in-progress poems with the class. Together, notice the way various groups describe the same thing with very different words and phrases.

- Copy the poems on large chart paper and display them where everyone can see them. Take pictures of the students exploring the globs of Oobleck. Display the pictures with their list poems.

STRATEGY 19

Science Sentence Poems

Scientists and poets are close observers of their world. Sometimes just a sentence can capture the poetic essence of a subject. Encourage students to start with something small and arrange it in different ways.

"But I Can't Write Poetry!"

Marilyn: When I meet students who say they can't write poetry, I start with sentence poems. I do this because in a matter of minutes, I have a room filled with new poet voices. The sentence poems they create are lovely beyond their length. I show students the authenticity of sentence poems by reading numerous examples, such as "A Writing Kind of Day":

> It is raining today,
> a writing kind of day.
>
> Each word hits the page
> like a drop in a puddle
> and starts off a tiny circle
>
> of trembling feeling
>
> that expands from the source
> and slowly fades away . . .
>
> —Ralph Fletcher (Yolen 1993b)

We also examine several poems by Arnold Adoff, Valerie Worth, and Lilian Moore to see how their poems look written out as sentences. We note the way poets place words on the page to illustrate or emphasize their meanings. For example, we look at the way Georgia Heard zigzags one sentence into a poem to suggest a hummingbird's movement in "Hummingbird":

> Ruby-throated hummingbird
> zig-
>   zags
>   from morning glories
> to honeysuckle

                    sipping
    honey
                from a straw
      all day long.

                —Georgia Heard (*Creatures of Earth, Sea, and Sky* 1992)

To begin our own sentence poems, I ask students to look out the window at the weather—rain, sun, falling leaves, snow, wind, ice. As a group we collaborate on building a sentence to describe what we see. After an ice storm one day, I ask for a sentence. This is what they give me:

    There was an ice storm.
    The ice storm covered every tree with ice.
    Every branch glittered with ice.
    As the sun began to shine, every branch glittered with ice.

We stop at this point and try out different line breaks:

    As the sun
    began to shine,
    every branch
    glittered
    with ice.

Writing sentence poems helps students see that poetry is not so different from regular language; its form makes it more dramatic. Teachers in my poetry workshop respond in the same way. They discover they can write sentence poems with great ease.

....

- Search for vibrant poems that are similar to sentences. Free verse is rich with examples.

- Write sentence poems collaboratively in a group. Expand and enlarge each sentence. For example: "The sun is shining. The sun is shining brightly. The sun is shining brightly through the trees. The sun is shining brightly through the trees and covers the ground with golden polka dots." Write it as a poem with different line breaks.

- Try different line breaks in sentence poems. Write and enlarge individual sentence poems.

- Expand ideas with phrases, adjectives, adverbs, and creative choices of words. Explore and practice.

Encouraging Students to Write Sentence Poems as They Explore Science

- Have students write their own poems after they create sentences as a group.

- Link sentence poems to a unit of study. If you are studying beaches, picture the beach and write about it. If students are writing animal reports, have them capture a quality of their animal. If they are reading biographies, have them discover the essence of their person. (See Strategy 25 for examples of poetry and biographies.)

- Conference with students to help them discover the most important things about their subject. Talking helps them to articulate the important qualities, the essence, that they can write about.

- Turn an incident into a poem. As an example, use "To Gentle Him" from Nancy Springer's *Music of Their Hooves* (1994): "He kicked me so hard his hoof left a bruise big as a plate."

S T R A T E G Y   2 0
Science Riddles

When we clothe concepts in language that we create, they become ours. Labeling an ephemeral thought or rehearsing something with words helps us to own it—it makes it ours. Putting concepts into language helps us to establish the concepts in our minds.

Fiddling with Science Riddles

Ginnie: My sixth-grade students create a web to show the interdependence between marine organisms and their environment. We list underwater land forms; a variety of weather and water variables; and a few immutables, such as the sun and the tides. Our web contains between fifty and sixty entries.

I ask pairs of students to create a riddle about any topic from the web. Delighted, they work secretly and rapidly; they astonish me with their results. Some of their riddles are a play on words:

What animal is found in the ocean,
and is also in the human body?

(Answer: a mussel/muscle)

Others show an understanding of some of the creatures and ideas we list:

> What can a whale hold
> but never touch?

(Answer: its breath)

> What can go up in the ocean
> but never come down?

(Answer: air bubbles)

We tease each other with our riddles for the remainder of the period. As the students leave to go back to their homerooms, they are still questioning each other. I post their riddles on the bulletin board; they are a focus in the classroom for weeks to come.

In the next class, we compare the way a riddle is written to the way other poems are written. For example, the poem "Lobster," in Joy Hulme's *What If?* (1993), describes the animal in a straightforward way—the title gives away the secret. If you know about lobsters, you can guess the answer. Other riddles encourage us to look at the familiar in new ways. They have the language of metaphor and simile:

> As round as an apple
>   As deep as a pail,
> It never cries out
>   Till it's caught by the tail.

(Answer: a bell) (Smith and Ra 1992)

During our next riddle session, we choose to focus on a common object such as a pencil, a safety pin, or a piece of chalk. We brainstorm about its qualities and functions before we create a riddle about it. This strengthens our observational skills. Here is one of the riddles:

> What leaves a trail
> Wherever it goes
> But the more it travels
> The smaller it grows?

(Answer: chalk)

Students need to have a solid understanding of concepts before they can begin to create their own riddles. When I ask them to guess the answer to a riddle, I give them plenty of time to understand it. Once they solve it, I ask, "Which words gave you the clues you needed? Which words were confusing when you first tried to figure it out?" This helps students to sort through the bulk of language to get to the core of meaning.

Introducing Science Riddles in Your Classroom

- Use riddles to introduce new topics or activities. Solving riddles gets students thinking about the content and scope of a unit.

- Find collections of riddles in the library or create some of your own. Look for *Behind the King's Kitchen* by William Jay Smith and Carol Ra (1992). For more complex concepts to solve, try *The Complete Book of Poems to Solve* by May Swenson (1993).

- Share riddles with your students to "prime the pump" and get them thinking about how riddles work. Chances are they will already know some familiar ones, such as "What's black and white and red [read] all over?" (Answer: a newspaper or an embarrassed zebra.) Ask students if they think a riddle is a poem. You'll get some interesting answers.

- Invite students to bring in riddles they know. Share your favorites with them. Riddles are games to play as well as poetry to enjoy. Once begun, riddling goes on for months.

- Model for students how to make riddles. Show that riddle shapers must choose their words carefully, giving clues to definitions without giving away too much. Demonstrate that when a riddle can have more than one answer, readers need another clue to help narrow the answer to one correct choice.

- Help students to notice that riddles have a form of their own. Unlike a dictionary, which gives the definition following a word, a riddle gives the definition first and the answer last. Riddles are mysterious; they give away just enough to require our thought if we are to solve them.

- Help students pare away unnecessary verbiage to get to the key words and phrases that leave a critical skeleton but don't give away the answer.

- Use riddles in all curriculum areas, including math, science, and social studies.

STRATEGY 21
Science Biographies

By reading biographies, students can visualize scientists as real people. When they write their own poems about scientists, they try to pick out the most important elements of a person's life. Poetry helps capture the essence of scientists' personalities and the motivations that drive them to their scientific work.

Ginnie: I want my fifth- and sixth-grade students to know and appreciate scientists as real people who struggle toward growth and knowledge, so I immerse them in literature about microbiologists' lives. We talk about the fabric and tension of the scientists' lives: what interests drive them, what ideas blossom and bear fruit, what handicaps block their way. Students look beyond factual information to imagine life in each scientist's time.

Since poetry helps us to focus on vivid moments and to use language with color and intensity, I ask students to use poetry to tell about the people who explore the world of microbes. First, students browse to choose a person as their subject. Then they read about that person in historical fiction, picture books, poetry, informational books, and biographies. I do not want them to rely only on the encyclopedia. I ask them to look for important events in the scientists' lives, either good or bad, and to think about what those times must have meant to the people who lived in them. Students write paragraphs to tell about those events. We have a conference about what they write to make sure that the important discoveries and moments of truth are there.

When I am sure that the students understand what the scientists' lives stood for, I know they are ready to turn their paragraphs into poetry. As we reread the paragraphs, we discuss peeling away unnecessary language but keeping vital phrases, and try putting in line breaks and testing how they affect the reader. We notice how punctuation causes a reader to pause and reflect, to stop and think. We search for language that tells our story with excitement and vigor.

I ask students to imagine how they would feel facing some of the roadblocks and frustrations the people of science faced. Encyclopedias don't always provide the depth of detail we need for this appreciation. I urge

Searching for Microbiologists in Poetry

students to search other information systems, adding what they know and looking for nonfiction that includes the area of study. For example, in our study, we explore many breakthroughs made in microbiology and we see a surge of discoveries made during the mid- and late-1800s. This inspires us to look further into that time span to find out why there was so much scientific interest and what was motivating research. We find that new inventions open doors to make it possible for people of vision to seek new answers.

Helping Students Move from Biographies to Poems

- Incorporate poetry with biographies in any subject area you examine. Read a biography aloud and compose a group poem about the person. Invite students to each give you one fact they know about a famous scientist. List these facts on the board. As a group, try different arrangements of lines until you achieve a satisfactory poetic statement. For example, here is a draft of a group poem in which students have listed facts about Marie Curie:

> Marie Sklodowska, born in Warsaw
> Traveled to Paris
> Studied chemistry and physics
> Worked with and married Pierre Curie
> Found uranium ore radioactive
> Discovered polonium and radium
> Shared the Nobel Prize in 1903
> First woman to get Nobel Prize
> Received another Nobel in 1911
> Died of cancer
> Could it be the radioactive ore?

In this case, students begin with a straightforward list of biographical facts but raise a foreboding question at the end. Help students to move beyond the factual list toward poetry by asking, "What moments in the person's life really stand out? What did the person do to change the world or the way we look at the world?"

- Encourage students to isolate critical events and the feelings that accompany them; this becomes the heart of a poem. As an example, use Brod Bagert's poem "Madame Curie's Biography":

> I wondered what she was like
>   at school.

Was she well behaved or bad?
Was she always happy,
Or was she sometimes sad?

Then, when I read a book about her,
I could see she was a lot like me,
And I felt a voice from deep inside . . .
    could it be . . .
Oh, could it really be?

—Brod Bagert (Cullinan and Galda 1994, 287)

- Ask students to highlight the "ah ha!" moments, the discouragements, and the persistent efforts of their subjects as they read.

- Ask students to write their poems from the point of view of their subjects, as though they are the scientists, inventors, explorers. This requires putting themselves into their subjects' shoes—imagining how they would feel during the experiences they write about.

- Give students who want to make their poems rhyme a rhyming dictionary, such as Marvin Terban's *Time to Rhyme* (1994). When students can't find words to fit a couplet or verse ending they often are tempted to bend the facts to make the poem work. They may lose interest and intensity for the sake of rhyme. Help them turn lines around, but assure them that meaning is most important. When a poem begins to lose its potency just to fit a rhyme pattern, it's time to abandon the rhyming effort and move to free verse.

Social Studies

Every cultural group has its poetry and songs; these are powerful ways to enter a culture and gain a sense of what a cultural group values. In 1863, Artemus Ward said, "Let me write the songs of a nashun [sic] and I don't care a cuss who goes to the legislature." He knew that the power of songs was far greater than any legislative acts. Decades later, as our nation focused attention on civil rights issues, many of us followed Martin Luther King, Jr., singing "We Shall Overcome." The strategies described in the following section intend to help students gain a sense of cultures through poetry and songs. They are: Cultural Heritage and Reading Poetry; Poetry Maps; Class Albums; Biography and Poetry; and Build Concepts in Social Studies.

S T R A T E G Y   2 2

Cultural Heritage and Reading Poetry

Children have a cultural heritage and a literary heritage; they need access to both. Cultural heritage includes the traditions, stories, and songs of ancestors; these become family folklore. Literary heritage resides in the stories members of a culture write; the literary traditions; and the stories people in that culture read, tell, or dramatize.

We live in a global culture aware that what happens any place in the world affects us all. When astronauts traveled to the Moon, they saw the Earth as a big blue marble, a rather small dot in a world of technology and jet travel. Daily newscasts underscore the message that we are all connected.

Children need information that leads to knowledge; this undergirds humanity and supports our hope for peace in the world. But information is not enough. Part of both cultural and literary heritage resides in poetry; children deserve to know it. They learn by hearing, reading, and writing poetry.

Studying Native American Culture and Poetry

Marilyn: The fourth-grade curriculum in our school includes a study of Long Island Indians, and the fifth-grade curriculum covers American Indians in other regions of the United States. I use poems from Terry Allen's *The Whispering Wind: Poetry by Young American Indians* (1972) to make connections between Indian tribes and areas of the country. I introduce the poem "Celebration," by Alonzo Lopez (Strickland 1993), as we study western groups.

Celebration

I shall dance tonight.
When the dusk comes crawling,
There will be dancing
    and feasting.
I shall dance with the others
    in circles,
        in leaps,
            in stomps.

Laughter and talk
    will weave into the night,

Among the fires
   of my people.
Games will be played
And I shall be
   a part of it.

—Alonzo Lopez

I copy the poem on chart paper, then students read it aloud. Some read alone; others choose parts and read it together. As we begin our study of Native Americans with the joy of Alonzo Lopez's poetic celebration, we become a part of it.

I immerse groups of students in the study of Native American culture by handing out copies of four or five poems by or about Native Americans and asking the groups to choose one to read or dramatize for their classmates. They explore the possibilities of one voice as narrator with others acting out the poem, choral reading, or giving lines to each student and taking turns reading. When they read *Hiawatha,* by Henry Wadsworth Longfellow (1983), one group adds instruments for the whispering of the pine trees; the lapping of the water; and the firefly, Wah-wah-taysee. Through sharing the readings and dramatizations, students begin to understand the poetry, concepts, and traditions of a culture.

Students soon discover that the spoken word was sacred for Native Americans. Grandparents and tribal elders passed down stories, prayers, lullabies, and songs to their young through spoken words and picture symbols. They relied on memory to preserve the important values of their culture, singing about the origins of the universe and providing advice to boys and girls. Reading poetry about other cultures allows our students' minds to travel to the four corners of the universe, too.

In a study of the Southwest, the fifth graders move back and forth between poetry and prose and also view some videos of the Southwest. We read Native American poetry and Scott O'Dell's books *Sing Down the Moon* (1970) and *Streams to the River, River to the Sea* (1986). Although we do not study the form of Native American poetry per se, students absorb its rhythms and style.

One student, Chris, says he cannot write a poem, but he begins to try reluctantly. It soon becomes clear that he has internalized the rhythm of the Native American voice and the essence of their beliefs. This is his poem:

I am running eagle
I fly through the sky
Like a general
Spying on the ocean
And mountain
No more can I spy

No more flying like
A general
No more land, tree and
My people
That spy on me.

—Chris

Students are often surprised and pleased with what they do. Chris
says, "That's the first good poem I ever wrote."
Sara writes about peace:

The Peace

The peace was once beautiful
  trees swayed
  birds chirped
then white man came with
  fancy engines
and now peace is no more.

Leah's poem is called "The Eagle":

The eagle is a mighty bird.
With wings of thunder,
eyes of lightning
And a body that
rises above the rest.

Figure 11 shows Leah's picture of the Indian sign for eagle.
Colleen's poem is longer than those of her classmates. She tells me in
our conference that this poem "just happened" and that it is a poem she
wanted to write, not one she had to write.

I Look Up

I look up,
and see the sky above.
Look down,
and see the ground.

I look to my left,
and see trees.
Look to my right,
and see a lake.

> I look up,
> and see a loving father.
>   Look down,
> and see a loving mother.
>
>   I look all around,
>   and see the life,
> that the rain god gave to me.

Teachers can use their personal readings to enhance professional preparations. I keep a journal for quotes or notes from books that I may want to refer to easily. The following quote is from *Wisdomkeepers: Meetings with Native American Spiritual Elders* (Wall and Arden 1990):

> Harriet Starleaf Gumbs, a tribal spokeswoman, states: "We give
> thanks to the Creator for these fruits of the sea. We ask his blessings
> on the food that we eat and on all the generations that follow us down

FIGURE 11. Leah's picture of the Indian sign for eagle.

to the Seventh Generation. May the world we leave them be a better one that was left to us." (47)

Poetry can help us to continue these traditions.

Sharing Poetry and
Cultural Heritage
with Students

- Immerse students in a culture through a variety of source materials, including poetry, prose, contemporary and historical fiction, nonfiction, picture books, and newspaper and magazine articles. After a thorough study, encourage them to write about the essence of a culture.

- Gather books of Native American writing; have students read and share excerpts and poems. Look for *The Whispering Wind* (Allen 1972), *Dancing Tepees* (Sneve 1989), *The Trees Stand Shining* (Jones 1971), and *Whirlwind is a Ghost Dancing* (Belting 1974, o.p.).

- Have students dramatize poems by sharing lines or stanzas. Suggest that they vary solo voices with group voices to enhance meaning.

- Collect photo essays; newspaper and magazine articles; informational books; and historical fiction, such as Scott O'Dell's *Streams to the River, River to the Sea* (1986) and *Sing Down the Moon* (1970), for students to use as source material. Take notes as you read. Copy favorite poems, passages, and traditions. Share with your students how you organize the quotes and poems you collect. Read aloud from the outstanding literature.

- Encourage students to explore a variety of ways to respond to the study. Some projects may result in picture books, travel brochures, poetry anthologies, original stories and poetry, letters, diaries, and news articles. They may result in a class album, a dramatization of a meaningful event, or a song.

- Collect photographs of areas your class studies. Have students match a poem with a picture on a bulletin board or in a class album.

- Collect poetry that reflects the cultural group you are studying—poetry by and about members of the group.

- Ask students to search for poems that reflect their own cultural heritage. Ask them to interview parents, relatives, and friends to locate poems they knew as children.

- Make group or individual collections in "Memories from Childhood" booklets using the materials students gather.

- Make a patchwork quilt of memories. Have students ask relatives about a family memory. Students can draw or embroider a patch for a group patchwork quilt. A parent who sews could help to put it together.

• Write a poem together about the heritage and customs of the people of a region or a culture.

• Read Monica Gunning's *Not A Copper Penny in Me House* (1993) to students. Identify the topics she chose to write about. Discuss what topics to write about in the culture your class is studying.

• Ask students to organize a collection of poems about their own culture. Categories might include celebrations, families, food, and holidays.

• Generalize ideas to other cultural groups. Find comparable categories such as foods, memorable events, literature, celebrations, country of origin, language, and family patterns. Make a comparison chart across cultural groups.

STRATEGY 23

Poetry Maps

Maps serve as a way to organize information and poetry about the world. Literature set in distant places helps us to develop a sense of place. In order for children to understand a story, they need to understand its setting. Mapping helps to develop that understanding.

Marilyn: I tell my students that when I thought of social studies as a child, I thought of large volumes of facts to memorize and mostly forget. Now, as a teacher of social studies, I think of maps, charts, graphs, globes, books, newspapers, magazines, videos, field trips, and poetry. Where does poetry fit into social studies? Everywhere! Poetry was around before the written word as elders passed down wisdom and culture (social studies) to their young.

I also tell my students how I feel about maps and about the role maps play in social studies. Maps allow us to become explorers of place, time, and history. The beauty of history shines in an ancient map and the beauty of discovery shines in a new one. I read to them from Beryl Markham's *West with the Night* ([1942], 1983):

Making Maps Meaningful

A map says to you, "Read me carefully, follow me closely, doubt me not." It says, "I am the earth in the palm of your hand...." Here is your map. Unfold it, follow it, then throw it away, if you will. It is only paper. It is only paper and ink, but if you think a little, if you pause a moment, you will see that these two things have seldom joined to make a document so modest and yet so full with histories of hope and sagas of conquest. No map I have flown by has ever been lost or thrown away; I have a trunk containing continents. (245–46)

I run my fingers over the lines of maps to show how I feel about them. I show my students that I want to plan trips and travel the red and black roads to places near in our community, and far into our country, continent, or world. I locate a spot on a map and read them a poem set in that country. As I point out Jamaica, for example, I read them "The Corner Shop" from Monica Gunning's *Not a Copper Penny in Me House* (1993, 10):

> "Chil', me stone broke," Grandma sighs.
> "Not a copper penny in me house.
> Go tell Maas Charles at the corner shop
> I want to trust a pound of codfish
> and two pounds of rice.
> I'll pay him when the produce dealer
> buys me dried pimento crop in season."
>
> Maas Charles never says no.
> He knows everyone in the village
> by their first names.
> He scoops from his bin, weighs and wraps,
> adds to his credit sheet on the wall
> a new amount under Grandma's name.
>
> Grandma always says,
> "Thank God for Maas Charles."

My students ask for map puzzles and maps to lay out on a table and explore. They try out poems about maps. Wouldn't it be fun to "map" poems? Why not have a poetry map? The map could be constantly changing, full of poems about weather, cultures, and landforms.

To begin our poetry map, we watch weather maps on the news. We talk about how our lives revolve around weather. It determines play—sleds or surfboards. It determines place—inside on a rainy day or outside picnicking under the sun. And it determines how people make a living in the area—selling lemonade or hot chocolate. As students read poetry books, they copy and collect weather poems, adding them to the poetry map. The

FIGURE 12. Poetry map.

map changes as the weather and seasons change. They copy Langston Hughes's "April Rain Song" from *The Dream Keeper* (Hughes 1986), and Ralph Fletcher's "A Writing Kind of Day" (Yolen 1993b).

I mount a big map of the United States on a bulletin board; students place a copy of a poem where they think it belongs. They decide, for instance, that Carl Sandburg's "Fog" (Yolen 1993b) belongs in Maine. They place a Navajo poem in Arizona. They put poems about Seminole Indians and the Everglades in Florida. They put Diane Siebert's "Heartland" (1989) in the Midwest. They put one copy of Lilian Moore's "Until I Saw the Sea" (Moore 1982, 53) on the East Coast, and another on the West Coast. They put snow poems in Minnesota. They put subway poems in New York, Boston, and Washington, D.C. The map remains on the board for months and is a repository for many poems (see Figure 12).

Some students want to try writing poems about maps even though I do not ask them to do so. Jeremy begins by listing what maps are, what they show, and what they tell as ideas:

> Maps are ink on paper
> Maps are lines in blue
> Maps are dots and circles
> Maps help dreams come true.

Maps show rivers and mountains
Maps show oceans and shores
Maps show towns and villages
Maps help open doors.

Maps show states and countries
Maps show a coming storm
Maps show a river forest
Maps help us find the warm.

Maps tell ancient history
Maps tell about the earth
Maps tell of the future
Maps help me know life's worth.

All the activities with maps and poems help my students feel more at ease with both. They use maps more frequently and include poetry in their reports more often.

Introducing All Kinds of Maps in Your Classroom

- Map weather poems. Assign weather poets or poetry map-keepers to choose from a collection of poems and keep the map up-to-date. As they read to select, they see a variety of topics and styles.

- Map cultures. Ask students to search for poems written by or about other nationalities and place them on a world map. Use Jane Yolen's *Street Rhymes Around the World* (1992) and *Sleep Rhymes Around the World* (1994b) to locate commonalities in the street games children play and in the lullabies parents sing to children around the world.

- Map landforms. Ask students to search for poems about rivers, mountains, lakes, prairies, deserts, and rain forests to place on maps.

- Map animals. Place animal poems in spots to represent their native lands. Map migration routes. Use poems to map habitats of endangered species, such as "Migration," "Elephant Warning," and "Whale Chant," all from Georgia Heard's *Creatures of Earth, Sea, and Sky* (1992). Use Barbara Esbensen's *Words with Wrinkled Knees* (1986) to identify animals from various parts of the world. Place the poems in appropriate spots on the map.

- Use a map of the United States as a continuing project of finding poems about people, animals, weather, or landforms from various regions. Put the poems—or titles of poems—on the map.

STRATEGY 24
Class Albums

Teachers who share personal experiences with their students demonstrate that they are human beings who also have families, joys, and heartaches of their own. Poetry can bring out a person's true emotions. Students recognize the authenticity of a teacher's response.

Ginnie: I am impressed with the poetry and photographs Marilyn shares with the fifth graders as we study Native Americans; I use her idea to organize photographs I took during a trip with my sons to the Grand Tetons and Yellowstone National Park. On each page of our album, I mingle poetry and lines from our trip journal with the pictures. The words give the album a richer texture and a deeper feeling than the pictures alone would give. I spend several wonderful hours searching for just the right poem to convey our appreciation of open space and our wonder at the wildlife and scenic beauty we enjoy. I also include poems that speak of the fun we had together.

Visiting Yellowstone and the Grand Tetons

I bring the album to school to share with my students. I want them to see how the album is organized so that we can make similar albums as we take field trips and do laboratory experiments. For our unit on Oceanography—Oceans Around the World—the students are delighted to type up their observations, find or create poetry, and write captions. The result serves as a personal reminder to the students—a memento that shows how much they learned and the aspects of the study that impress them.

Mixing Pictures and Poetry in Your Classroom

- Plan a photographic record of a unit of study. Take pictures of journeys you make that are related to the study. Include pictures of artifacts, models, paintings, and the class group at work on their projects. Invite students to take pictures, too. Combine the photographs into one album or have students create individual ones.

- Have students search through poetry books and anthologies for selections to enhance the photographs. Encourage them to look for poems that give them the sense of "Oh, yes! That's just the way I feel, too!"—as well as for those that give information.

- Use the notes students take and their journal or log entries to create captions and stories about the pictures. These can be handwritten or typed. Cut the written entries to fit the spaces around the photographs.

- Cut some of the pictures into varied shapes (stars, circles, ovals, free form) to add interest to the album.

- Encourage students to use snippets of information taken from their reading and research. A group of two or three can write a paragraph about one aspect of the study. Use the paragraph as it is or help the authors turn it into a poem by experimenting with line breaks, margins, punctuation, and language (see Strategy 11).

- Encourage students to compose their own poetry for the album to describe their feelings and experiences.

- When a group album is complete, give every student a chance to take it home to share with family. Include a response sheet:

    We read the class album together. We think _____.
    Signed (Family member) _____.

- Keep the class album in a special place for frequent readings. Books created in class are the ones students most often want to read and reread.

- Try to persuade your students to donate the album to the school media center at the end of the school year. That way, they and others can check it out again and again as they progress through the grades.

....

STRATEGY   25
Biography and Poetry

In an attempt to provide children with a set of heroes to emulate, biographers of earlier days wrote only about the good qualities of their subjects. Contemporary biographers, however, are more likely to show a realistic picture of the person, both negative and positive. Biographies help children develop an understanding of historical periods and the people who contributed to them. Poetry enhances that understanding of the people and the times.

Ginnie: During Black American History month, our fifth- and sixth-grade students read biographies of famous African Americans. After they read a biography, they write a paragraph about the trials, accomplishments, and essence of their subject. Then they distill their thoughts from the paragraph into a few words that ring with truth, thorough knowledge, and regard. This is a poem Candace writes while we are studying Black History:

················
Celebrating Black History Month

Queen Mother Moore

> She Cried
> She cried
> She cried
> She felt the
> Lash on the
> Backs of
> Her people
> She never
> Cried
> So
> Much
> In
> Her
> Life.

Ann chose Arthur Ashe:

Ashe Himself

Ashe, a kind loving caring person.

A person that wanted everyone to be treated equally, no matter what he or she had to do,

The first black man who had to work hard to win Wimbledon,

A person who didn't want his color to matter whether he or anyone else was red, green, or purple,

> A person who didn't want
> anyone's color to keep their
> dreams from coming true.

Someone who had to accomplish something in his life.

Arthur Ashe.

The poem sings with conviction. It shows clearly how the student identifies with her subject and understands what motivated him.

- Have students search for poems about people they study.

- Ask students to use poetry to respond to what they read.

- Encourage students to compose poems as if they were characters from the biographies, writing to describe an event from the subject's point of view.

- Model for students the process of distilling the essence of an editorial, news article, filmstrip, or video. Use the "Think Aloud" technique—say out loud what you are thinking and considering as you make decisions. After the students observe you, do a Think Aloud together as a large group activity. Then ask students to do one in small groups, later with a partner, and finally, individually.

- Show students how to identify important ideas and feelings in a selection. Help them search for the kind of language that best carries the message they want to convey.

- Ask students to write a paragraph or two about a person from history. After they have written the paragraph, help them pare it down into a poem (see Strategy 11 for techniques).

- Ask students to write a paragraph about the theme of your current unit study. Through conferences and sharing periods, determine whether they grasp the meaning of the theme or the readings. If so, encourage them to write a poem.

STRATEGY 26
Build Concepts in Social Studies

Historical fiction, biography, nonfiction, poetry, art, and music help students build a framework for understanding historical periods and social studies concepts. Teachers who move from traditional textbooks to literature-based programs sometimes fear they won't cover all the "facts" students need to know. Some make a checklist of key concepts from textbooks and the social studies curriculum. They help students build concepts from as many different vantage points and through as many means as they can. Poetry plays an important role because it presents dramatic feelings, clear images, and vivid settings in brief, impactful texts. Students remember historical periods if they have a framework of stories, vivid images from poetry, and information from many sources (Wooten 1991).

Ginnie: When I teach the sixth-grade unit on the historical period from the turn of the century, World War I, and the Great Depression, I start with Claudia Lewis's *Long Ago in Oregon* (1987) and *Up in the Mountains and Other Poems of Long Ago* (1991) to help students build a foundation of understanding about the way life was lived during that period. Claudia Lewis's poems are like miniature snapshots in a photograph album, describing the family life and activities of a young girl in a small town in Oregon during 1917 and 1918. The poet describes her excitement when she hears the sounds of a wood saw from a sawmill and tells about her fright when she sees farmers throw snakes into a bonfire to make the grass safe. She describes the foreboding and fears generated by the threat of World War I. My students relate to her feelings even though the time period is ancient history to them. They remember the imagery from this selection of poems and can visualize the settings. The poems establish a foundation for seeking further information.

Discovering the Past Through Poetry

Helping Students Explore History Through Poetry

- Have students collect poetry that describes the historical period to be studied. Poems about early America, the Westward Movement, or families help students connect with these subjects more personally.

- Search for poems about people who lived during the historical period you study (e.g., Abraham Lincoln or Nancy Hanks).

- Have students work collaboratively or individually to find poems about well-known historical figures. Display copies of the poems as you study the related period. Have students search for poetry about the past.

- Create a poetry time line together of the years studied. Draw a line on the chalkboard or on poster board and write the years of events you have studied in class. Work from the past to the present. Find poems that correspond to the time frames of the events and place them under the dates on the time line.

Math

The trend toward an integrated curriculum has had its impact on teaching mathematics. Math educators now define their field not as isolated practice and memorization of equations but as problem solving—thinking mathematically and practicing skills in context. Teachers use math in an integrated curriculum. For example, in a study of animals, students go to a zoo, make graphs of the amount of food animals eat, determine the ratio of food to body size, draw maps of the zoo, estimate miles to the zoo, and estimate the amount of food the zoo keepers use daily. Although they use math textbooks and informational books primarily, they use stories and poetry, too.

STRATEGY   27
Poetry and Math

When teachers think of their curricular responsibilities, they include language arts, social studies, science, and math. Increasingly, teachers use trade books, photo essays, picture books, and reference books in social studies and science, but they don't use them as readily in math. Many continue to think of math as numbers while they think of other curriculum areas as words.

Making Acrostics in Math

Marilyn: I help students understand that math consists first and foremost of words. Math is vocabulary. It is pervasive in all that we do and know. Every math problem we encounter involves sentences and stories, even if what we see is reduced to an equation.

I use Shel Silverstein's poem "Smart" in *Where the Sidewalk Ends* (1974) to teach the concept that math is language. This poem also brings a little humor into math class. It is about a child who trades one dollar bill for two quarters, then three dimes, then four nickels, and finally five pennies. Each time he makes a trade he thinks he has gained money because he has more pieces of it. However, he doesn't understand the value of each piece. I use Carl Sandburg's poem "Arithmetic" (1993) to bring laughter to a subject that some children take as deadly serious. Both poems help students

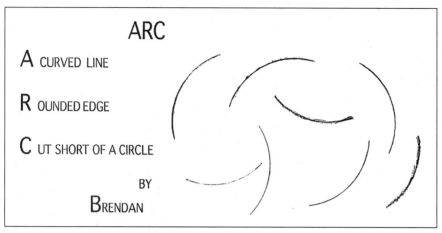

FIGURE 13. Brendan's "Arc" poem.

see math as language. Once they make this connection, I let them play around with words to form poems. The following acrostic poems were done in Jean's sixth-grade math class. Figure 13 shows Brendan's poem. In Figure 14, Nicolas used an acrostic to express his frustration. Figure 15 shows Stephanie's acrostic.

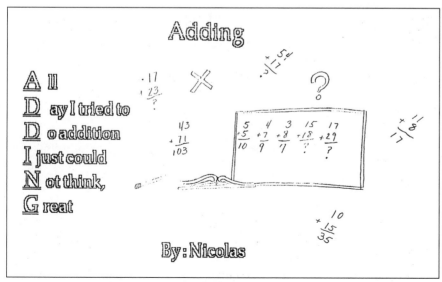

FIGURE 14. Nicolas's acrostic poem "Adding."

MATH

Math is

A fascinating subject

The problems

Have interesting solutions

FIGURE 15. Stephanie's poem "Math."

Helping Students Recognize the Connection Between Language and Math

- Ask your students to use a recent copy of the *Guinness Book of World Records* (McFarlan 1991) to locate the fastest runner, swimmer, or skier. Ask them to find the distance covered and the amount of time used, determine the miles per hour the athlete moved, and incorporate the information into a poem about the record holder.

- Involve your students in *Anno's Math Games* (Anno 1987) to see if they understand the concepts and can solve the problems. Challenge them to create similar games modeled on the ones Anno portrays. Ask the students to write a poem about things that can be measured and those that cannot.

- Introduce Louis Sachar's *Sideways Arithmetic from Wayside School* (1989). Ask students to locate some of the math problems in Wayside School that are similar to ones in your school. Encourage students to describe them in poems.

- Introduce Louis Phillips's book, *The Upside Down Riddle Book* (1982). Ask students to use some of the math riddles as models for writing their own.

- Make a classroom collection of street and jump-rope rhymes that include numbers. Illustrate them and bind them into a classroom anthology.

STRATEGY 28
Write to Learn Math

Today's math lessons often begin with a story containing a problem that must be solved through a mathematical process. Some books, such as Pat Hutchins's *The Doorbell Rang* (1986), include plots that revolve around a math problem. In Hutchins's book, for example, children must divide a batch of cookies equally as the number of guests changes. As teachers read such books to the class, they invite students to propose as many different ways to solve the problem as possible. Working together, they try out each suggestion and evaluate its efficiency and accuracy. They discover that there are different ways to arrive at the right answer.

Ginnie: Karen slouched into our fifth-grade classroom one morning with her shoulders slumped and her eyes on the ground. She walked over to my desk and dropped an envelope on it without meeting my eye. Then she turned and went to her desk. "Oh, oh," I thought, "something's up at home."

I was right—the note was from Karen's mother. There had obviously been a big scene the night before when Karen couldn't do her math homework. "How," asked Karen's mother, "can Karen build on concepts and skills that she doesn't seem to understand in the first place?"

After reading the note, I thought about Karen's quiet manner during math instruction. She followed all I said and did carefully, but she was hesitant about answering questions and almost never volunteered. She could do the work in class, but not at home. What was missing for her?

Up to this point, I still had been finding my way to using writing to teach math. I had asked students to do very little writing in math. To tell the truth, I wasn't sure just how to begin, or what to ask of them. After receiving that note, however, I sought help from our Math Coordinator, professional journals, and books such as Joan Countryman's *Writing to Learn Mathematics* (1992). I began to use math journals as a way for children to explore thinking about mathematics. I introduced double-entry journals: on one side of the page students work out the math equation; on the other side, they explain what they are doing and thinking. At the end of each problem, they write about what they are feeling. I find that having the kids write in math serves the dual purpose of letting me see where they are and

Learning to Like Math Through Poetry

where their difficulties lie. I also discover how they are feeling about math; the writing gives them an outlet to express their thoughts and concerns.

One activity the students especially enjoy is creating poetry about math. I find through their writing that Karen's problem is not unique. I find statements like these: "I guess this is right." "I can't figure out how to get this done." "I don't even understand the problem and I sure don't know how to get the answer." Students need more than instruction and guided practice to internalize the concepts and skills we teach. They need to make the language of process, logic, and ideas their own. They need to rehearse this language, to share it out loud and on paper. And they need an opportunity to examine for themselves, without censor, the way they think and feel about the world of numbers.

Another student, Sal, expressed vehement feelings in his math journal: "I hate it. I hate it. I'm a dummy. I have a calculator, why do I need to learn how to multiply? I don't want to remember the multiplication tables. They stink but maybe someday I'll need them." Later Sal wrote his feelings out in different ways. Finally he put them in this form:

> I hate math, I hate math, I hate math
> What good will it do?
> I'll have a secretary
> I'll have a calculator
> I'll have a computer
> But who will watch my money?

Through writing about math in journals and poems, Sal was able to come to terms with his negative feelings, exploring on his own the reasons why "maybe someday" he'll need math.

Helping Students Explore Math Through Poetry

- Share poetry about math and arithmetic with your class. Carl Sandburg's *Arithmetic* (1993) and *One Hundred Hungry Ants* by Elinor J. Pinczes (1993) are good resources. Also try *You Know Who* by John Ciardi (Ciardi 1991b) and "A Math Lesson" from *Upside Down and Inside Out* by Bobbi Katz (1992).

- Ask students to write about an area of math that is difficult or easy for them. Once children get used to writing about math, they become comfortable sharing their feelings about failures and successes. Share the paragraphs if authors are willing. Other children need to know that they are not alone in their struggles with fractions, division, etc.

- Talk with students about how trying to solve word problems makes them feel. Encourage them to incorporate these feelings in revisions of their paragraphs. Work with the pieces by abstracting the essence and considering line breaks to make them look like poetry on a page (see Strategy 11).

- Suggest to students that the themes of poems can include questions, unclear thoughts, explanations, definitions, likes and dislikes, reflections about a lesson, connections between math ideas and life, comparisons, surprises, predictions, and "I wonder" statements.

- Use math journals as a source for poetry about math. Have students search for phrases and ideas that seem suitable for a poem. Tell them to look for strong feelings, imaginative ideas, and creative ways of expressing a thought or a procedure. Lift phrases from journals and discuss where they might fit into a poem. Ask, "Are these beginnings or endings? What else do you want to say about this?"

- Write limericks about math in groups of two so students can discuss ideas and understandings. Writing and talking helps them to clarify their thinking.

- Post student poems about math on a bulletin board, publish them in a group anthology, and add them to personal collections. Children's magazines such as *Scholastic Dynamath, Scholastic Math,* and *3-2-1 Contact* publish student submissions. Addresses for ordering and information about the contents of these magazines can be found in *Magazines for Kids and Teens: A Resource for Parents, Teachers, Librarians, and Kids!* (Stoll 1994).

. . . .

STRATEGY 29

Time, Poetry, and Problem Solving

Children's concepts of time and chronology do not develop well until they are about eleven years old—until they can succeed on Piaget's tests of conservation (for example, that two containers of different shapes can hold the same amount of water). Before they reach this age, students have difficulty keeping a sense of sequence, historical periods, and cause and effect on historical events in mind. Time lines provide an opportunity for students to put order into their thinking.

Marilyn: I ask students to create a time line when they need help with sequencing, chronology, and historical periods. I start the time line around the classroom wall and ask students to add to it. At some point, I bring in an old Sears and Roebuck catalog from the year 1902 and ask them to figure out how much it would cost to buy their school clothes at 1902 prices. I ask them to describe the way they would dress, choosing only from the old mail-order catalogs.

I read them David McCord's poem "No Present Like the Time," found in *One at a Time* (McCord 1977, 420–21):

> "No time like the present," they always used to say,
> Meaning—*Busy! Do You Hear Me? Don't Delay!*
> Much better in reverse (it doesn't have to rhyme):
> Simply, simply, *No present like the time.*
>
> Time, you agree, is everybody's gift,
> But the packages aren't the same.
> The lid of each is there to lift,
> Yet only one package bears your name.
>
> Lift the lid a little now each morning,
> And what comes whistling out?
> A day's supply of time. Almost a-borning
> It dies with every breath as you go about
>
> Your work or play. How much of it is in
> That package? No one knows. You, least of all.
> Time is indifferent to what we begin;
> Indifferent also to whether we stand or fall.
>
> "Don't waste your time," they say. Waste time you will;
> And such as you wish, of course, is yours to squander.
> Don't call it wasted when you climb a hill!
> Through fields and woods to wander
>
> Is to be young, and time belongs to the young.
> It's when you're old that clocks begin to tick.
> Play fair with time: his praise so rarely sung.
> He is your snail. But oh, his pulse is quick.

David McCord plays with language by reversing a timeworn aphorism—no time like the present—and gives the phrase a totally new meaning—that time to squander is a gift. Knowing that McCord was born in 1897 and that he is ninety-seven years old now adds a sense of pathos to the phrase "It's when you're old that clocks being to tick."

- Ask students to create a time line of their own lives. Have them search for and include poems that remind them of different stages in their lives.

- Encourage students to write about how it feels for time to pass when they are waiting for a special holiday, when it is a school vacation, when they are visiting someone. Have them search for poems that express impatience about time moving slowly or surprise at its moving rapidly.

- Search for poems as a group that reflect different historical periods. For example, look at the poems of A. A. Milne (1924) and Robert Louis Stevenson (1905). Ask students, "How do the poems reflect life at that time? Do the children in the poems behave the same way you do?"

The Arts: Visual Art, Drama, and Music

The National Endowment for the Arts (1988) states that a basic arts education comprises four major disciplines: literature, visual art and design, performing art, and media art. A thorough grounding in these four areas helps students make informed critical choices.

Poetry is especially useful in the arts. It blends easily with music and song, translates readily into scripts for performance, and combines happily with art. Its resources are adaptable to the related field of the arts. Students reveal their understanding by interpreting stories and poetry through visual art, drama, and music.

Visual Art

Visual art is a good companion to poetry. Both use representational thinking—they use one thing to represent another. For example, when a child uses a wooden block to represent a car, he or she is using representational thought. Representational thought is imaginative thought and is the basis for analogies, metaphor, and symbols.

Art, specifically visual art, is an excellent way to communicate across cultures. We may not understand others' verbal language, but we will most likely understand their artistic forms of expression. In effect, art is another language; it extends our first language.

Samantha, a thirteen-year-old student with special needs, was able to enter emotionally into the paintings done by a local artist. By feeling what it would be like to live in the spaces created by the artist, Samantha expressed herself in poetry. Her book, *Reach for the Moon* (Abeel 1994), is an excellent way to introduce the concept of combining poetry and art. It is also an example of the strengths of a child with special needs.

Art, Music, and Poetry

Poetry, music, art, dance, and movement are all symbolic languages. Examine one topic across all forms of expression. For example, in a study of trees, use the popular World War I song, "Don't sit under the apple tree with anyone else but me"; read Joyce Kilmer's poem "I think that I shall never see . . . a poem as lovely as a tree" (Ferris 1957); study the way artists portray trees; dance and sway to music to demonstrate how trees blow in the wind; impersonate trees that can move to imitate the people who walk past them.

. . . .
Drawing to Music and Poetry

Ginnie: When I taught nursery school, we would play music while the children painted or drew pictures. Consistently, Tchaikovsky's music evoked sweeping lines and curves with a sense of ballet movement across the page. Stravinsky's music brought out bold colors and angular images of modern dance. Although children could not describe in words the way the music made them feel, they could show us on paper.

Now when I introduce a poem to students in grades three through six, I remember those very young children and their ability to *show* rather than *tell* what a musical image means. Because poetry and music are both strong, symbolic languages, I include painting and drawing among the techniques available for student expression and response. Students can choose line, form, and color to express the impact of a poet's words.

One day, to expose my students to different kinds of poetry, I hand out construction paper and tell them I will read six poems. The first time they are just to listen and to picture the setting. During the second reading, they are to choose a poem and to begin drawing. My selections are mostly about nature; they are poems by ancient Japanese and Korean poets in the forms of tanka and sijo, forms that predate haiku. They are poems I love. The beauty of the poems slips into the students as easily as their crayons slip across the paper.

Students often say to me, "I could just see it in my mind." "I know exactly what the poet means, because that's the way I feel, too." I look at the intensity of their artwork to sense how they have understood the heart of the poem.

• Ask students, "How can you draw the way the poem makes you feel? What colors and shapes remind you of that feeling? How will you use the space to show feelings?"

• Make paper, paint, crayons, markers, and other art supplies available for students to express their response to poems. When they complete their drawings, have them share and talk about what they drew and where their ideas came from.

• Help students to move beyond a literal visualization of exactly what the poem says. Encourage them to express the feelings they get from the poem instead. Use "Where We Ride To" (Springer 1994) to pull listeners beyond the horse and rider to the bigger landscape and feelings of openness and freedom.

• Read some of your favorite poems aloud several times without showing the poems or any illustrations to the students. Ask them to draw the essence of what they hear. Your voice will reveal your feelings and your interpretation of the poet's words.

• After sharing the poem aloud, let them see it on paper. The way a poet shapes a poem is part of its power and vision.

• Display a chart or poster of a poem and place students' artwork around it.

• Find picture-book poems and look at ways different artists illustrate them. Compare Robert Frost's unillustrated poems in anthologies with *Stopping by Woods on a Snowy Evening* illustrated by Susan Jeffers (1990), *Birches* illustrated by Ed Young (1988), and *A Swinger of Birches: Poems of Robert Frost for Young People* illustrated by Peter Koeppen (1982). See *Talking to the Sun: An Anthology of Poems for Young People* (Koch and Farrell 1985) for illustrated poetry and songs. Check *Go in and Out the Window: An Illustrated Songbook for Children* by the Metropolitan Museum of Art Staff (1987) to view classical paintings from the Metropolitan collection chosen to illustrate favorite song poems. Compare Susan Jeffers's illustrations for Henry Wadsworth Longfellow's *Hiawatha* (1983) and for Chief Seattle's letter in *Brother Eagle, Sister Sky* (Jeffers 1991). Byrd Baylor has written several story poems about the Southwest illustrated in picture books by Peter Parnall. Compare his illustrations in Baylor's *Desert Voices* (1981), *Everybody Needs a Rock* (1974), *The Desert is Theirs* (1975), *Hawk, I'm Your Brother* (1976), *I'm in Charge of Celebrations* (1986), *The Other Way to Listen* (1978a), and *The Way to Start a Day* (1978b).

....

Drama

Dramatics is one of the language arts, a central one given the primacy of oral language, and yet it is given short shrift in many elementary classrooms. This is not the case with teachers who have discovered poetry, however. Teachers who feel confortable with poetry have a great advantage in a drama program. Poetry makes a drama program come alive. Once students and teachers find out how much fun it is to dramatize a poem, they want to do it often.

Not all poems are easy to dramatize, to say aloud, or to interpret orally. You begin to recognize kinds that work after you have tried a few. Poems that work well for performance have a dramatic voice and reveal some emotional conflict. You can assume the voice of the central character or speaker, and you know what kind of emotion to portray. Poetry and drama are natural partners (Bagert 1994).

STRATEGY 3 1
Storytelling and Cultures

Every group has its major poets who portray the essence of the culture. Reading poetry can be an excellent way to learn about a culture.

....

Meeting a Pueblo Storyteller

Marilyn: I tell students in grades three through six that in every culture there are storytellers who pass down values and specific traditions of a culture. In the late 1800s, storyteller Santiago Quintana worked with visiting anthropologists to maintain his culture's traditions (Bahti 1988, 7). Helen Cordero, Quintana's granddaughter, created a clay figure of a Pueblo man with five children on his lap and shoulders in memory of her grandfather. The figure of a Pueblo man with children climbing over him is becoming a contemporary symbol of storytellers.

Every generation hands down advice to its children. For example, Native Americans teach their children to have great respect for the earth and to value nature and its creatures. They believe that the land belongs to all people and do not think that an individual can "own" land. Together we read and discuss the advice that Native Americans have sung in the finest oral tradition to their children. It then seems logical to send students to their own elders for advice. My students interview their parents, grand- parents, and older people in their community. They ask, "What was one of the most important things you were supposed to learn when you were my age?" Students find that although much differs in various cultures, there is much that is the same.

Here is a poem I ask my students to read and discuss:

Foreigner

My papa is a foreigner
My mama is also a foreigner
Marianne and I are foreigners too
right now
though we're American

Because right now we're in England
Ha, ha!
Didn't think of that, did ya?
That Americans are foreigners too
as soon as they're out of the country

—Siv Widerberg in *I'm Like Me* (1974)

Understanding other cultures and reflecting on our own relationship to the world can contribute to world peace.

Parents, grandparents, relatives, and neighbors are all rich sources for storytelling, although it is often difficult to commit their tales to paper. My own efforts to chronicle family history include using a tape recorder and a camcorder, both of which render my parents speechless; and beginning a book, still largely unwritten, called "Grandmother Remembers." I finally realize that my mother's weekly letters are probably the best record of fam- ily history I will ever get or need.

Similarly, the personal narratives that students write daily in our class- rooms are family stories that should be treasured now and kept for the future. We are all storytellers.

. . . .

- Have students interview parents, grandparents, and older relatives for information about their culture that should be handed down to them and to future generations. Suggest that students ask for poems, say- ings, proverbs, and rules to live by that their relatives were taught.

Helping Students Learn About Cultural Heritage

- Invite grandparents to come to school to tell students stories about their childhood, school days, and youth.

- Encourage students to write narratives and poems about their lives and their family. Keep their writing in a folder or journal. Suggest categories such as celebrations, families, food, traditions, and holidays.

- Expose students to the storytelling of other cultures through poetry and narratives.

- Read aloud to your students *Not a Copper Penny in Me House* by Monica Gunning (1993) for a portrait of life in the Caribbean. Read *Families* (Strickland and Strickland 1994).

- Find poetry books that reflect specific cultures. For example:

  My Song is a Piece of Jade (de Gerez 1984): Toltecs of ancient Mexico.
  Beyond the High Hills (Rasmussen 1961): Eskimo.
  Out of the Earth I Sing (Lewis 1968): Eskimo, Polynesian, Aboriginal.
  A Coconut Kind of Day (Joseph 1990): Island Poems.
  The Seasons of Time (Baron 1968): Tanka poetry of ancient Japan.
  In a Spring Garden (Lewis [1965] 1989): Japanese.
  Sunset in a Spider Web (Baron 1974): Sijo poetry of ancient Korea.
  Unicef Book of Children's Poems (Kaufman 1970): Around the world.
  My Shalom My Peace (Zim 1975): Paintings and poems by Arab and Israeli children.
  The Moon is Like a Silver Sickle (Morton 1972): A celebration of poetry by Russian children.
  A Tune Beyond Us (Livingston 1970): Various cultures, with translations.
  Black Out Loud: Anthology of Modern Poems by Black Americans (Adoff 1970): Black Americans.

STRATEGY 32

Performance and Poetry

Children become poetry performers if we invite them to step gradually into the process. First, we as teachers need to perform a poem—we need to model the process for the students. Next, we invite students to recite a few poems as a group; this puts no one on the spot. Later, we can invite individuals to perform short poems. Finally, we can encourage individuals to recite poems of their own choosing. At all stages of the process, children are able to hold a copy of the poem in their hands—to use or not use as they wish. Poetry performance is not a memory test. Brod Bagert, poetry performer, says that if children make the right face as they say a poem, then everything falls into place (1992). He suggests we help students to search for what a poem means and to ask, "What face should I make when I say these words?" When we make a face to express feeling, we automatically give the right expression to the words.

Children who perform poetry and move to it remember it longer. When they voluntarily memorize a poem for performance, they make it their own for a lifetime. I can still recite the poems I learned by heart in elementary school.

Ginnie: As part of a teachers' workshop on using children's literature in language arts, five teachers, including myself, are creeping about on a rug. On hands and knees, we imitate snails while a poem is read aloud. Just as children would do, we act out every phrase of the poem, trying our best to look and feel "snailish." We live the words we hear.

Participating in Movement

Children have the ability to reach deeply inside themselves to probe an idea; they almost become a part of it. They do this when they pretend to be cowboys, elephants, or teachers. Authors do it, too. Many books and poems are written from an animal's or object's point of view, such as Joy Hulme's poems in *What If?* (1993). I like to bring young children close to poetry—to take them inside a poem by having them dramatize it and bring it to life. They capture the mood of a poem by acting it out, role playing, and dramatizing it.

Selecting Poetry to Perform

When you are searching for poems for students to perform, look for poems that:

speak with the child's voice
use lots of dialogue
tell a little story or episode
have closure or an ending that signals
  the end of the poem
contain emotion that the speaker
  can portray

Encouraging Students to Act Out Poems

- Choose a poem with possibilities for dramatization—one with action, strong feelings, and obvious intentions. Some good choices include *Casey at the Bat* by Ernest Thayer (1988), Barbara Esbensen's "Elephant" in *Words with Wrinkled Knees* (1986), "Pretending" in *Upside Down and Inside Out* by Bobbi Katz (1992), Jack Prelutsky's "Spaghetti, Spaghetti" in Kimberly Colen's *Peas and Honey* (1995), Brod Bagert's *Let Me . . . Be the Boss* (1992) and *Chicken Socks* (1994), and John Ciardi's "Mummy Slept Late and Daddy Fixed Breakfast" in *Time for Poetry* by Arbuthnot and Root (1968). Read the poem aloud—at least twice—with dramatic expression. Talk about the poet's words to develop a strong sense of the meaning before the students begin to move. Let students choose the parts they want to play. Have several children play the same part—this encourages shy participants who prefer not to be the sole attraction. Go through the performance several times. While the first run-through may be rather stilted, each succeeding performance shows arm, facial, and body movements becoming increasingly elaborate and free. As you observe these "drafts," tell the performers what you see in relation to the poem. For example, as I watch children perform Lillian Morrison's "The Sun" from *Whistling the Morning In* (1992), I see them going around the world in their movements—loosening up each time:

> Each evening
>   the sun
> goes on a journey
> under the world.
>
> Each morning
>   he returns
> a little weary
> having been through
> danger and dark places.
>
> We greet him with
> cheers and gratitude.
> He grows and glows
> for us, tall, taller.

I respond, "Jaime, I see the way your back is all bent over. You look so tired after your trip through the night!" and "Dorothy, I notice that you grow taller and taller at the end of the poem. Is your big smile the sun's glow? It makes me feel warm!" And it does.

- Search for poems that have animals, machines, mountains, or water. Students can "become" anything. Familiarize them with the poem before attempting to act it out. Their movements should flow from one line of action to another as they anticipate what is coming next. There is no "dead time." Rereading in rehearsal allows students to think ahead and plan how they will dramatize their subjects.

- Ask students to compare the ocean or a storm to a person. Invite them to use their imaginations and powers of observation to describe the phenomenon in a new way.

- Choose a poem involving several roles such as Isaac Olaleye's "Village Market" in *The Distant Talking Drum* (1995). Create scenes from the village market by having students play the roles of the women, children, goats, sheep, chickens, dogs, tortoises, and monkeys who surround the market.

- Use technical terms, such as *personification,* in your normal conversation about poetry, but don't try to teach these terms as isolated bits of knowledge. When you use a technical term, surround it with lots of examples from poetry and stories. Praise students when they cite examples.

- Use drama to jump-start students' enthusiasm for poetry. Tell students to close their eyes and imagine a big winter storm blowing into town (that does not take much imagination during a Long Island winter!). Tell them to give the storm a face. Ask if it's angry, sneaky, silent, having fun, looking for something to upset, or in a rush to get somewhere else. Have them write about the storm as it passes through town. Invite them to use he or she as they describe the storm. Help them turn their stories of the storm into poems by cutting out unecessary words, creating line breaks, using punctuation, and arranging the words differently on paper. Ask them to show the movements they write about. Add interesting new words to a Word Bank (group or individual) for writing.

> **Poems for Two Voices**
>
> Poems for two voices make excellent performance material. They can be read by groups or individuals. Here are some books that contain poems for two voices:
>
> *I Am Phoenix: Poems for Two Voices* (1985) and *Joyful Noise: Poems for Two Voices* (1988) by Paul Fleischman.
>
> *Creatures of Earth, Sea, and Sky* by Georgia Heard (1992).
>
> *Music of Their Hooves* by Nancy Springer (1994).

- Choose two contrasting poems, such as "Sandpiper" and "Fawn" from *A Hippo's a Heap* by Beverly McLoughland (1993). Help students adapt to the difference between a rollicking poem that invites them to dance and one that invites quiet contemplation. Whole body movement helps young children capture the mood of poetry. Talk about words and rhythms that suggest action. Help them to develop a vocabulary to describe the many moods of poetry.

- Help self-conscious older students to evolve in dramatization from simple hand and upper body movements toward whole body movement. Begin by having students draw a picture to represent the mood of a poem such as "Tropical Hurricane" in *Not a Copper Penny in Me House* by Monica Gunning (1993). Then encourage them to translate the drawings into action.

- Read dialogue between two persons or groups, such as "Fishes" or "Frog Serenade" from *Creatures of Earth, Sea, and Sky* by Georgia Heard (1992). Arnold Spilka's *Monkeys Write Terrible Letters* (1994) contains dialogue material:

Are you an elephant?
  I'm not sure.
Why aren't you sure?
  My mother never told me.
Was she an elephant?
  I don't know. What does an elephant look like?
An elephant is very large.
  I'm not sure if she was.
Did she have big floppy ears?
  I never noticed.
Did she have a large trunk?
  What is a trunk?
A trunk is a long winding nose that hangs down.
  I don't remember.
But elephants always remember!
  Then I guess I'm not an elephant.

Also use Nancy Springer's "Talking to the Horse Trainer" in *Music of Their Hooves* (1994).

"You been kicked?"
  "Yep."
"Did it hurt?"
  "Yep."
"You been bitten?"
  "Yep."
"That hurt too."
  "Uh-huh."
"Been run away with?"
  "Some days."
"Take a fall?"
  "Now and then."
"Get stepped on?"
  "Once."
"More than once."
  "That's true."
"How many times?"
  "Maybe twice."
"More than that."
  "What's your point?"
"Look at me."
  "Okay, I'm looking at you. So?"
"How come you still love horses?"
  "How come I still love you?"

Read Paul Fleischman's *Joyful Noise* (1988) and *I Am Phoenix* (1985). Each set of voices has different words to say and portrays different expressions and actions.

- Divide the class into groups of three or more students. Let each group select from books or sheets of poems available until they find one they want to perform. Have students read the selections several times to get an idea of the tone and intent they want to convey. Help them decide where two or more voices make an impression, where a feeling of strength is needed, where the mood seems solitary, where the sound of the words would be emphasized if spoken by three people instead of one person, and where the words need to be spoken quickly or slowly. After they practice and revise their presentation, have each group present their interpretation to the rest of the class. Invite the class to talk about what they see and feel in the performance and how the presenters achieved the effects they wanted.

- Ask students who have become adept in sharing poems written for two voices to present other poems as choral or dual readings. When different groups of students choose to present the same poem, discuss the fact that there is NO ONE RIGHT WAY to read a poem. Discuss which aspects of each presentation seemed most effective.

- Discuss how the students' own poetry could be presented in role playing and drama. Ask them to picture the topics of their poems as animated objects come to life. Ask them to show you in action what they describe on paper. Help them find action words to portray their subject. Dramatize it to keep it lively and visual.

. . . .

Music

Music is another form of language—another system of symbols used to communicate ideas. Music has been incorporated into all aspects of our life: our work, our play, and our religious observances. Every culture creates its own music, giving us a wide variety of sounds from all parts of the world. It gives us a means to communicate through sounds put together in special ways to express feelings and ideas in another form. For example, we transform a feeling about a rainy, dreary day into a chant "Rain, rain, go away. Come again another day." Soon it becomes a song, a melody that brightens our spirit.

Words set to music are called lyrics, and lyrics are a form of poetry. Many song lyrics become famous poems, and many poems are set to music to become songs. Poets and musicians use lyrics to say more than is immediately apparent to the senses. They compose to explore new meanings and to express something beyond the moment.

STRATEGY 33

Poetry and History in Songs

Students like to know the "inside story" on authors, illustrators, books, poems, or songs. Tell them the background about famous people or events to heighten their interest. This knowledge will impress their family and friends.

Singing Famous Songs

Marilyn: I tell my fourth- and fifth-grade students about Katherine Lee Bates standing at the summit of Pike's Peak, capturing its beauty, and writing the poem "America the Beautiful" (Ferris 1957). Later, Samuel A. Ward set it to music. Originally, we did not think of the song as a poem, but knowing its history now causes us to look at the words in a different way.

> O beautiful for spacious skies
> for amber waves of grain,
> for purple mountain majesties
> above the fruited plain . . .

I also tell students how Francis Scott Key immortalized another picture in poetry and music during the War of 1812; it became our national anthem. During the war, Key, a young lawyer, was sent aboard a British ship to negotiate the release of an American prisoner. He was held aboard the ship and overheard the British Admiral boasting that the American flag over the fort would not be there by morning; the British were planning to attack Fort McHenry that night. Key's poem tells how he listened to the sounds of battle and how grateful he felt when the flag was still there in the morning (Spier 1986). Knowing the origins of the song helps students to foster a new interest and respect for the words and the country they symbolize. In both these instances, a picture produced a poem that was set to music. By connecting these songs to history instead of just singing them by rote, we link poetry and social studies.

When my daughter was in fifth grade and studying the United States, her teacher's assignment for the students was to find songs about every part of America. To locate the songs, students ran to the library, searched through piano benches, and asked parents and grandparents. The teacher did not spend hours alone, nights and weekends, doing the research to execute her fine idea. She searched and learned along with her students; the end result was a shared effort. Parents smiled and tapped their feet to the familiarity of "Shenandoah," "Carry Me Back to Old Virginny," "Red River Valley," and "Erie Canal." The students were involved authentically and everyone got a lesson in the music of our American heritage. The students found history more relevant by learning about music, poetry, songs, and stories.

• Ask students to collect street songs and jump-rope rhymes such as "Red, white, blue, tap me on the shoe . . . ." Poetry is a natural language for children; they use it in their play as they jump rope and sing a rap song. They sing as they play tag, bounce balls, and swing on swings. Use Jane Yolen's book *Street Rhymes Around the World* (1992) to find songs from other cultures. Ask students to make a collection of their own songs and jump-rope rhymes.

• Have students collect folk songs that correspond to the historical period you are studying.

• Ask students to find poems that "sing to you." Michael R. Strickland says that you can think of his book, *Poems That Sing to You* (1993), as a soundtrack to take home from a favorite performance to enjoy again and again. He encourages the reader to mix a love for poetry with an appreciation of music.

• Look at history through music. Students can discover the "generation gap" by exploring poems about the history of music such as "The Piper," "A New Age," "Two Jazz Poems," and "Jazz Fantasia" (all in Strickland 1993). They can share and discuss a family's struggle to tolerate each other's musical preferences by reading "Umbilical," "Compact Disk," and "Rock 'N' Roll Band" (all in Strickland 1993). Brod Bagert suggests in "Wolfgang Rock" (Strickland 1993, 25) that the past may be more congruent with the present than we think:

> If Mozart were alive
> He'd be playing lead guitar,
> Dancing in the spotlight
> And prancing like a star.
> His hair would be dyed purple
> And his music would be bold.
> If Mozart were alive
> He'd be playing rock and roll.

Helping Students Connect Poetry and Songs

- Encourage students to make personal connections between music and poetry. Ask them to write down the lyrics for their favorite songs and tell how they relate to the words.

- Read poems simply for the music of the words. Read song lyrics as poems. Michael Strickland reminds us, "Read them twice: once for the words, and again for the music of the words" (Strickland 1993).

- Study the art and music in *Go In and Out the Window* (Metropolitan Museum of Art Staff 1987), a songbook illustrated with art from the Metropolitan Museum of Art collection. Songs such as "Clementine," "Oh! Susanna," and "Sweet Betsy from Pike" could be used in connection with a study of the Gold Rush. The art shown includes "Camp Fire" by Winslow Homer, a sculpture titled "The Mountain Man" by Frederic Remington, a watercolor and print of cowboys by Thomas Eakins, and "The Homestead" by Frederic M. Grant. Also see Peter Spier's illustrated books: *Erie Canal* (1990), *The Star Spangled Banner* (1986), and *The Fox Went Out on a Chilly Night* (1961).

- Discuss some of the following items if your students have enough experience to understand the composition of a song or poem: Does the song/poem have a special beat or rhythm to it? How can you tell? Why do you think the poet created the line breaks and left the white spaces where they are? Is the punctuation unusual? Where? Did we do anything different when we were reading the poem or singing the song because of the punctuation or line breaks? What kinds of decisions do you think the author of this poem or song might have made while writing it?

- Save the poem after you share it, and hang it where students can read it whenever they wish. Don't just make poetry available, make it unavoidable.

- Jane Yolen celebrates the music that water makes in *Water Music* (1995b). She says that she hears melodies that water sings across the rocks. Her son took photographs of water in all its forms, and Jane Yolen wrote poems that the pictures suggested to her. Try a similar idea. Collect photographs or cut pictures from magazines that suggest poems to you. Paste your poems beside the pictures. Laminate or put plastic wrap over the pages to preserve them.

Summary

This book describes ways to help children develop a love of poetry. It is based on the idea that the more familiar we are with a subject, the better we will like it. That is, the more children know about poetry, the more they will like it. The strategies described here are ones that come from real class-rooms with real teachers and real children. The strategies are launching pads for teachers to try out and move beyond. The strategies suggest ways to integrate poetry throughout the curriculum and make it part of every child's life.

Poetry readers become poetry writers. Children's imaginations are fresh and clear—they see things in images and often speak in poetic ways. Kornei Chukovsky (1963) noted children's use of figurative language when he studied Russian children's language development. Chukovsky calls children linguistic geniuses because of the repeated inventiveness in their images. One child said that a bald man had a "barefoot head," and that the husband of a grasshopper was a "daddyhopper." They create new words like a poet. We want to take advantage of a child's use of images and help them expand this kind of imaginative thinking into all that they do.

Poets themselves advise young students to read a lot, copy poems that please them, jot down images they think of, and copy interesting words or phrases that appeal to them. They tell students to make language their toy, their plaything, and a source of pleasure. When this happens, students have accepted the invitation to poetry. And teachers have come, too, to celebrate the joys of poetry in all that they do.

Epilogue

We say that poetry is important because it has beautiful language, creates vivid images, and helps us see the world in a new way. But it is also important for another reason—it helps us to remember.

Fifteen years ago I taught a course on CBS television called Sunrise Semester. The subject was the critical reading of literature, and I interviewed many famous writers of children's literature including Isaac Asimov, Katherine Paterson, Madeleine L'Engle, Judy Blume, Mary Rodgers, Paul Zindel, Maurice Sendak, and many others.

One day, I did a program on poetry with a young doctoral student, Steve Kussin, who taught seventh- and eighth-grade students in Brooklyn. That day Steve brought video clips from his classroom. When he announced to his students "Today, we're going to do poetry," a clamor arouse. "Yuck!" "No way!" "Boo!" "Get outta here!" Steve asked, "Do you like songs? Well, a song is a poem set to music."

Steve turned to his cassette recorder and played Simon and Garfunckel's "Sounds of Silence." The students responded with enthusiasm "That's more like it!" "Yeah, that's good." They listened to the song a couple of times, and Steve said "Every single thing that poets do to make us notice words is in that song." He proceeded to make a chart of the literary devices—the vehicles poets use to make language memorable—used in the song:

> personification
> onomatopoeia
> simile
> metaphor
> paradox

After the students had been through the song several times, they were comfortable with the terminology and said, "Oh, I didn't know that's what you were talking about." "Yes, I see what that means."

Steve's homework assignment was for the students to take another Simon and Garfunckel song and do the same thing—search for the literary devices in it. Later, they picked any song they liked and did the same thing. They wrote their own poetry. They performed their own poems as songs.

I tell Steve's story here because of the effect it had on the teachers and graduate students who watched that show and took the course. Wherever I go, people say to me, "I used to watch you on television. I got up at 6:00 A.M. to see you. Remember that teacher who did the poetry? I've never forgotten that show."

Was it the poetry? Yes, of course it was. Was it Steve's creative teaching idea to take something familiar to his students and turn it into new learning? Yes, it was that, too. The dynamic combination of poetry in the hands of a creative teacher is what we want for all students. I hope this book helps make that happen.

Professional References

Anderson, R. C. 1978. "Schema-directed processes in language comprehension." *Cognitive psychology and instruction.* Ed. A. Lesgold et al. New York: Plenum.

———. 1994. "Role of the reader's schema in comprehension, learning, and memory." *Theoretical models and processes of reading.* Ed. R. B. Ruddell et al. Newark, DE: International Reading Association.

Anderson, R. C., and P. David Pearson. 1982. "The new buzz word in reading is schema." *Instructor magazine* 91: 46–48.

Anderson, R. C., J. W. Pichert, and L. L. Shirey. 1979. "Effects of the reader's schema at different points in time." (Tech. Rep. No. 119). Urbana, IL: University of Illinois, Center for the Study of Reading (ED 169 523).

Anderson, R. C., R. J. Spiro, and M. C. Anderson. 1978. "Schemata as scaffolding for the representation of information in connected discourse." *American educational research journal* 15: 433–40.

Bagert, Brod. 1992. Promotional material presenting Brod Bagert. Honesdale, PA: Wordsong/Boyds Mills Press.

Bahti, Mark. 1988. *Pueblo stories and storytellers.* Tucson, AZ: Treasure Chest Publications, Inc.

Benton, M., J. Teasey, R. Bell, and E. Hurst. 1988. *Young readers responding to poems.* London: Routledge.

Benton, M., and G. Fox. 1985. *Teaching literature: Nine to fourteen.* London: Oxford University Press.

Booth, David, and Bill Moore. 1988. *Poems please! Sharing poetry with children.* Markham, Ontario: Pembroke Publishers Limited.

Calkins, Lucy. 1990. *Living between the lines.* Portsmouth, NH: Heinemann.

Cambourne, Brian. 1987. "Language, learning and literacy." *Towards a reading-writing classroom,* Andrea Butler and Jan Turbill. Portsmouth, NH: Heinemann.

Chukovsky, Kornei. 1963. *From two to five.* Ed. and trans. Miriam Morton. Berkeley, CA: University of California Press.

Cisneros, Sandra. 1991. "Eleven." *Woman Hollering Creek and other stories.* New York: Random House.

Countryman, Joan. 1992. *Writing to learn mathematics.* Portsmouth, NH: Heinemann.

Cronemeyer, Elizabeth. 1993. "Chemistry for kids." *Booklinks* Vol. 2, No. 6.

Cullinan, B. E., and L. Galda. 1994. *Literature and the child, 3d edition.* Fort Worth, TX: Harcourt Brace College Publishers.

Fox, Mem. 1993. *Radical reflections.* San Diego: Harcourt Brace.

Harste, Jerome C., Kathy G. Short, and Carolyn Burke. 1988. *Creating classrooms for authors: The reading-writing connection.* Portsmouth, NH: Heinemann.

Harwayne, Shelley. 1992. *Lasting impressions: Weaving literature into the writing workshop.* Portsmouth, NH: Heinemann.

Heard, Georgia. 1989. *For the good of the earth and sun: Teaching poetry.* Portsmouth, NH: Heinemann.

Heimlich, Joan E., and Susan D. Pittelman. 1986. *Semantic mapping: Classroom applications.* Newark, DE: International Reading Association.

Just, M. A., and P. A. Carpenter. 1980. "A theory of reading: From eye fixations to comprehension." *Psychological review* 87: 329–54.

Lewis, Richard, ed. 1968. *Out of the earth I sing.* New York: W. W. Norton.

McVitty, Walter, ed. 1992. *Word magic: Poetry as a shared adventure.* Rozelle, Australia: Primary English Teaching Association.

National Endowment for the Arts. 1988. *Toward civilization: A report on arts education.* Washington, DC: National Endowment for the Arts.

Rumelhart, D. E., and J. L. McClelland. 1980. *An interactive model of the effect of context in perception.* Part 2: CHIP Tech. Report. La Jolla, CA: University of California, Center for Human Information Processing.

Sebesta, Sam. 1988. *Poems please! Sharing poetry with children,* D. Booth and B. Moore. Markham, Ontario: Pembroke Publishers Limited.

Steffensen, M. S., C. Joag-Dev, and R. C. Anderson. 1979. "A cross-cultural perspective on reading comprehension." *Reading research quarterly* 15: 10–29.

Stoll, Donald, ed. 1994. *Magazines for kids and teens: A resource for parents, teachers, librarians and kids!* Newark, DE: International Reading Association and Educational Press Association.

Sutherland, Zena, and M. C. Livingston. 1984. *The Scott, Foresman anthology of children's literature.* Glenview, IL: Scott, Foresman.

Thiele, Colin. 1992. *Word magic: Poetry as a shared adventure.* Ed. Walter McVitty. Rozelle, Australia: Primary English Teaching Association.

Wall, Steve, and Harvey Arden. 1990. *Wisdomkeepers: Meeting with Native American spiritual elders.* Hillsboro, OR: Beyond Words Publishing, Inc.

Whitin, D. J., and S. Wilde. 1992. *Read any good math lately? Children's books for mathematical learning, K-6.* Portsmouth, NH: Heinemann.

Wooten, Deborah. 1991. "The use of historical fiction trade books in collaboration with social studies textbooks and its relation to learning in the social studies classroom." Ph.D. diss., New York University.

Children's Books

Abeel, Samantha. 1994. *Reach for the moon.* Illus. Charles R. Murphy. Duluth, MN: Pfeifer-Hamilton Publishers.

Adoff, Arnold, ed. 1970. *Black out loud: Anthology of modern poems by Black Americans.* New York: Dell.

———. 1973. *Black is brown is tan.* Illus. Emily A. McCully. New York: HarperCollins.

———. 1979. *Eats: Poems.* Illus. Susan Russo. New York: Lothrop.

———. 1982. *All the colors of the race.* Illus. John Steptoe. New York: Lothrop.

———. 1986. *Sports pages.* Illus. Steve Kuzma. New York: Lippincott.

———. 1988. "Interview with Arnold Adoff." Promotional material. San Diego: Harcourt Brace.

———. 1989. *Chocolate dreams.* Illus. Turi MacCombie. New York: Lothrop.

———. 1990. *Hard to be six.* New York: Lothrop.

———. 1991. *In for winter, out for spring.* Illus. Jerry Pinkney. San Diego: Harcourt Brace.

Ahlberg, Janet, and Allan Ahlberg. 1979. *Each peach pear plum.* New York: Viking.

Allen, Terry, ed. 1972. *The whispering wind: Poems by young American Indians.* Garden City, NY: Doubleday.

Anno, Mitsumasa. 1987. *Anno's math games.* New York: Philomel.

Arbuthnot, May Hill, and Shelton Root, Jr. 1968. *Time for poetry.* 3d ed. Illus. Arthur Paul. Glenview, IL: Scott, Foresman.

Bacmeister, Rhoda W. 1976. "Galoshes." In *The Arbuthnot anthology of children's literature.* 4th ed. Ed. Zena Sutherland et al. New York: Lothrop.

Bagert, Brod. 1992. *Let me be . . . the boss.* Illus. G. L. Smith. Honesdale, PA: Wordsong/Boyds Mills Press.

———. 1994. *Chicken socks and other contagious poems.* Illus. Tim Ellis. Honesdale, PA: Wordsong/Boyds Mills Press.

Baron, Virginia Olsen, ed. 1968. *The seasons of time.* New York: Dial

———. 1974. *Sunset in a spider web.* New York: Henry Holt.

Bates, Katherine. 1957. "America the beautiful." *Favorite poems old and new.* Ed. Helen Ferris. Illus. Leonard Weisgard. New York: Doubleday.

Baylor, Byrd. 1974. *Everybody needs a rock.* Illus. Peter Parnall. New York: Scribner.

———. 1975. *The desert is theirs.* Illus. Peter Parnall. New York: Scribner.

————. 1976. *Hawk, I'm your brother.* Illus. Peter Parnall. New York: Scribner.

————. 1978a. *The other way to listen.* Illus. Peter Parnall. New York: Scribner.

————. 1978b. *The way to start a day.* Illus. Peter Parnall. New York: Scribner.

————. 1981. *Desert voices.* Illus. Peter Parnall. New York: Scribner.

————. 1986. *I'm in charge of celebrations.* Illus. Peter Parnall. New York: Scribner.

Becker, John. 1985. *Seven little rabbits.* Illus. Barbara Cooney. New York: Scholastic.

Belting, Natalia. 1974. *Whirlwind is a ghost dancing.* Illus. Leo and Diane Dillon. New York: Dutton. o.p.

Brinckloe, Julie. 1985. *Fireflies.* New York: Macmillan.

Brown, Margaret Wise. 1979. *The little fir tree.* Illus. Barbara Cooney. New York: HarperCollins.

Cannon, Janell. 1993. *Stellaluna.* San Diego: Harcourt Brace.

Carlstrom, Nancy White. 1986. *Jesse Bear, what will you wear?* Illus. Bruce Degen. New York: Macmillan.

Chase, Edith N. 1986. *New baby calf.* Illus. Barbara Reid. New York: Scholastic.

Children in Theresienstadt Concentration Camp. [1964] 1993. *I never saw another butterfly.* New York: McGraw-Hill.

Ciardi, John. 1967. "Mummy slept late and daddy fixed breakfast." In *Time for poetry.* 3d ed. Comp. M. H. Arbuthnot and Shelton Root, Jr. Chicago: Scott, Foresman.

————. 1985. *Doodle soup.* Illus. Merle Nacht. Boston: Houghton Mifflin.

————. 1989. *The hopeful trout and other limericks.* Illus. Susan Meddaugh. Boston: Houghton Mifflin.

————. 1991a. *The monster den.* Illus. Edward Gorey. Honesdale, PA: Wordsong/Boyds Mills Press.

————. 1991b. *You know who.* Illus. Edward Gorey. Honesdale, PA: Wordsong/Boyds Mills Press.

————. 1993. *Someone could win a polar bear.* Illus. Edward Gorey. Honesdale, PA: Wordsong/Boyds Mills Press.

————. 1994. *The reason for the pelican.* Illus. Dominic Catalano. Honesdale, PA: Wordsong/Boyds Mills Press.

Cisneros, Sandra. 1991. "Eleven." *Woman Hollering Creek and other stories.* New York: Random House.

Colen, Kimberly. 1995. *Peas and honey: Recipes for kids (with a pinch of poetry).* Illus. Mandy Victor. Honesdale, PA: Wordsong/Boyds Mills Press.

Cullinan, Bernice E. ed. 1995. *A jar of tiny stars.* Illus. Marc Nadel and Andi MacLeod. Honesdale, PA: Wordsong/Boyds Mills Press.

cummings, e. e. 1987. *Little tree.* Illus. Deborah Kogan Ray. New York: Crown.

de Gerez, Toni, adapt. 1984. *My song is a piece of jade: Poems of ancient Mexico in English and Spanish.* Boston: Little, Brown.

de Paola, Tomie. 1985. *Tomie de Paola's Mother Goose.* New York: Putnam.

de Regniers, Beatrice Schenk. 1983. "Keep a poem in your pocket." *The Random House book of poetry for children.* Select. Jack Prelutsky. Illus. Arnold Lobel. New York: Random House.

————. 1988. *Sing a song of popcorn.* New York: Scholastic.

Delacre, Lulu. 1984. *Arroz con leche: Popular songs and rhymes from Latin America.* Select. and illus. Lulu Delacre. New York: Scholastic

Domanska, Janina. 1987. *If all the seas were one sea.* New York: Macmillan.

Einsel, Walter. 1962. *Did you ever see?* Illus. by author. Reading, MA: Addison-Wesley.

Esbensen, Barbara. 1986. *Words with wrinkled knees.* Illus. John Stadler. New York: HarperCollins.

———. 1992. *Who shrank my grandmother's house?* Illus. Eric Beddows. New York: HarperCollins.

Farjeon, Eleanor. 1984. *Eleanor Farjeon's poems for children.* New York: HarperCollins.

Ferris, Helen. 1957. *Favorite poems old and new.* New York: Doubleday.

Fleischman, Paul. 1985. *I am phoenix: Poems for two voices.* Illus. Ken Nutt. New York: Harper-Collins.

———. 1988. *Joyful noise: Poems for two voices.* Illus. Eric Beddows. New York: HarperCollins.

Fletcher, Ralph. 1991. *Water planet.* Paramus, NJ: Arrowhead Books.

Frost, Robert. 1982. *A swinger of birches: Poems of Robert Frost for young people.* Illus. Peter Koeppen. Owings Mills, MD: Stemmer House.

———. 1988. *Birches.* Illus. Ed Young. New York: Henry Holt.

———. 1990. *Stopping by woods on a snowy evening.* Illus. Susan Jeffers. New York: Dutton.

Galdone, Paul. 1983. *The gingerbread boy.* Illus. Paul Galdone. New York: Clarion.

———. 1986a. *Over in the meadow.* Illus. Paul Galdone. Englewood Cliffs, NJ: Prentice-Hall.

———. 1986b. *Three little kittens.* Illus. Paul Galdone. New York: Clarion.

Goldstein, Bobbye. 1992. *Inner chimes.* Illus. Jane Zalben. Honesdale, PA: Wordsong/Boyd Mills Press.

Greenfield, Eloise. 1978. *Honey, I love, and other love poems.* Illus. Leo Dillon and Diane Dillon. New York: HarperCollins.

Guarino, Deborah. 1989. *Is your mama a llama?* Illus. Steven Kellogg. New York: Scholastic.

Guiberson, Brenda Z. 1991. *Cactus hotel.* Illus. Megan Lloyd. New York: Henry Holt.

Gunning, Monica. 1993. *Not a copper penny in me house.* Illus. Frané Lessac. Honesdale, PA: Wordsong/Boyds Mills Press.

Harrison, David. 1993. *Somebody catch my homework.* Illus. Betsy Lewin. Honesdale, PA: Wordsong/Boyds Mills Press.

Hart, Jane. 1982. *Singing Bee!* Illus. Anita Lobel. New York: Lothrop.

Heard, Georgia. 1992. *Creatures of earth, sea, and sky.* Illus. Jennifer Dewey. Honesdale, PA: Wordsong/Boyds Mills Press.

Heller, Ruth. 1981. *Chickens aren't the only ones.* New York: Putnam.

Henkes, Kevin. 1991. *Chrysanthemum.* New York: Greenwillow.

Hoberman, Mary Ann. 1978. *A house is a house for me.* Illus. Betty Fraser. New York: Viking.

———. 1981. *Yellow butter purple jelly red jam black bread.* Illus. Chaya Burstein. New York: Viking.

———. 1991. *Fathers, mothers, sisters, brothers.* Illus. Marylin Hafner. Boston: Little, Brown.

Holbrook, Sara. 1995. *Nothing's the end of the world.* Honesdale, PA: Wordsong/Boyds Mills Press.

Hopkins, Lee Bennett. 1974. "My Name." In *Kim's place.* New York: Holt, Rinehart. o.p.

———. 1984. *Surprises.* Illus. Megan Lloyd. New York: HarperCollins.

———. 1987. *More surprises.* Illus. Megan Lloyd. New York: HarperCollins.

———. 1993a. *Beat the drum: Independence Day has come.* Illus. Tomie de Paola. Honesdale, PA: Wordsong/Boyds Mills Press.

———. 1993b. *Easter buds are springing: Poems for Easter.* Illus. Tomie de Paola. Honesdale, PA: Wordsong/Boyds Mills Press.

———. 1993c. *Good morning to you, Valentine: Poems for Valentine's Day.* Illus. Tomie de Paola. Honesdale, PA: Wordsong/Boyds Mills Press.

———. 1993d. *Merrily comes our harvest in: Poems for Thanksgiving*. Illus. Ben Shecter. Honesdale, PA: Wordsong/Boyds Mills Press.

———. 1993. *Ragged shadows: Poems of Halloween night*. Illus. Giles Laroche. Boston: Little, Brown.

———. 1995. *Hand in hand: American history in poetry*. New York: Simon & Schuster.

Hughes, Langston. 1986. *The dream keeper and other poems*. New York: Knopf.

Hulme, Joy N. 1993. *What if?* Illus. Valeri Gorbachev. Honesdale, PA: Wordsong/Boyds Mills Press.

Hutchins, Pat. 1986. *The doorbell rang*. New York: Greenwillow.

Jackson, Holbrook, ed. 1951. *The complete nonsense of Edward Lear*. New York: Dover Publications.

Jarrell, Randall. 1967. *The bat poet*. Illus. Maurice Sendak. New York: Macmillan.

Jeffers, Susan. 1991. *Brother Eagle, Sister Sky: A message from Chief Seattle*. Illus. Susan Jeffers. New York: Dial.

Jones, Hettie. 1971. *The trees stand shining*. Illus. Robert Andrew Parker. New York: Dial.

Joseph, Lynn. 1990. *A coconut kind of day*. New York: Lothrop.

Katz, Bobbi. 1992. *Upside down and inside out*. Illus. Wendy Watson. Honesdale, PA: Wordsong/Boyds Mills Press.

Kaufman, William E., ed. 1970. *Unicef book of children's poems*. Harrisburg, PA: Stackpole Books.

Koch, Kenneth, and Kate Farrell. 1985. *Talking to the sun: An anthology of poems for young people*. New York: Henry Holt.

Kuskin, Karla. 1959. *Just like everyone else*. New York: HarperCollins.

———. 1980. *Dogs and dragons, trees and dreams*. New York: HarperCollins.

———. 1985. *Something's sleeping in the hall*. New York: HarperCollins.

———. 1987. *Jerusalem, shining still*. Illus. David Frampton. New York: HarperCollins.

———. [1956] 1991. *Roar and more*. New York: HarperCollins.

———. 1992. *Soap soup*. New York: HarperCollins.

Larrick, Nancy. 1968. *Piping down the valleys wild*. New York: Delacorte.

———. 1974. *Room for me and a mountain lion: Poetry of open space*. New York: M. Evans and Company.

Lewis, Claudia. 1987. *Long ago in Oregon*. Illus. Joel Fontaine. New York: HarperCollins.

———. 1991. *Up in the mountains and other poems of long ago*. Illus. Joel Fontaine. New York: HarperCollins.

Lewis, Richard, ed. 1968. *Out of the earth I sing*. New York: W. W. Norton.

———. [1965] 1989. *In a spring garden*. Illus. Ezra Jack Keats. New York: Dial.

Little, Jean. 1971. *Kate*. New York: HarperCollins.

———. 1987. *Little by little: A writer's education*. New York: Viking.

———. 1989. *Hey, world, Here I am!* New York: HarperCollins.

Livingston, Myra. 1970. *A tune beyond us*. New York: Macmillan.

Lobel, Arnold. 1981. *On market street*. Illus. Anita Lobel. New York: Greenwillow.

———. 1984. *A rose in my garden*. Illus. Anita Lobel. New York: Greenwillow.

Longfellow, Henry Wadsworth. 1983. *Hiawatha*. Illus. Susan Jeffers. New York: Dial.

Manley, Molly. 1994. *Talkaty talker: Limericks*. Illus. Janet Marshall. Honesdale, PA: Boyds Mills Press.

Markham, Beryl. [1942] 1983. *West with the night*. San Francisco: North Point Press.

Martin, Bill, Jr. 1983. *Brown bear, brown bear, what do you see?* Illus. Eric Carle. New York: Holt.

———. 1991. *Polar bear, polar bear, what do you hear?* Illus. Eric Carle. New York: Holt.

Mathews, Louise. 1978. *Bunches & bunches of bunnies.* Illus. Jeni Bassett. New York: Putnam.

McCord, David. 1977. *One at a time: His collected poems for the young.* Illus. Henry B. Kane. Boston: Little, Brown.

McFarlan, Donald. 1991. *Guinness book of world records.* New York: Bantam.

McLoughland, Beverly. 1993. *A hippo's a heap.* Illus. Laura Rader. Honesdale, PA: Wordsong/Boyds Mills Press.

Merriam, Eve. 1964. *It doesn't always have to rhyme.* Illus. Malcolm Spooner. New York: Atheneum.

———. 1986. *Fresh paint.* Illus. David Frampton. New York: Macmillan.

Metropolitan Museum of Art Staff. 1987. *Go in and out the window: An illustrated songbook for children.* New York: Henry Holt.

Milne, A. A. 1924. *When we were very young.* New York: E. P. Dutton.

———. 1927. *Now we are six.* New York: E. P. Dutton.

Moon, Pat. 1991. *Earth lines: Poems for the green age.* New York: Greenwillow.

Moore, Lilian. 1982. *Something new begins.* New York: Atheneum.

Morrison, Lillian. 1992. *Whistling the morning in.* Illus. Joel Cook. Honesdale, PA: Wordsong/Boyds Mills Press.

Morton, Miriam, ed. 1972. *The moon is like a silver sickle: A celebration of poetry by Russian children.* New York: Simon & Schuster.

O'Dell, Scott. 1967. *The black pearl.* Boston: Houghton Mifflin.

———. 1970. *Sing down the moon.* Boston: Houghton Mifflin.

———. 1986. *Streams to the river, river to the sea.* Boston: Houghton Mifflin.

Olaleye, Isaac. 1995. *The distant talking drum: Poems from Nigeria.* Illus. Frané Lessac. Honesdale, PA: Wordsong/Boyds Mills Press.

Paladino, Catherine, select. and illus. 1993. *Land, sea & sky: Poems to celebrate the earth.* Boston: Little, Brown.

Panzer, Nora, ed. 1994. *Celebrate America: In poetry and art.* New York: Hyperion.

Parnall, Peter. 1986. *Winter barn.* New York: Macmillan.

Paterson, Katherine. 1978. *The great Gilly Hopkins.* New York: HarperCollins.

Peek, Merle. 1988. *Mary wore her red dress & Henry wore his green sneakers.* Illus. Merle Peek. New York: Clarion.

Phillips, Louis. 1982. *Upside down riddle book.* New York: Lothrop.

Pinczes, Elinor J. 1993. *One hundred hungry ants.* Boston: Houghton Mifflin.

Prelutsky, Jack. 1983. *Zoo doings: Animal poems.* Illus. Paul Zelinsky. New York: Greenwillow.

———. 1983. *The Random House book of poetry.* Illus. Arnold Lobel. New York: Random House.

Rasmussen, Knud, ed. 1961. *Beyond the high hills.* Cleveland, OH: World Publishing Co., Inc.

Rawls, Wilson. 1961. *Where the red fern grows.* New York: Doubleday.

Rees, Ennis. 1993. *Fast Freddie Frog.* Illus. John O'Brien. Honesdale, PA: Wordsong/Boyds Mills Press.

Rylant, Cynthia. 1982. *When I was young in the mountains.* Illus. Diane Goode. New York: Dutton.

———. 1990. *A couple of kooks.* New York: Orchard.

Sachar, Louis. 1989. *Sideways arithmetic from Wayside School.* New York: Scholastic.

Sandburg, Carl. 1993. *Arithmetic.* Illus. Ted Rand. San Diego: Harcourt Brace.

Sendak, Maurice. 1986. *Chicken soup with rice.* New York: HarperCollins.

Seuss, Dr. 1949. *Bartholomew and the Oobleck.* New York: Random House.

Siebert, Diane. 1988. *Mojave.* Illus. Wendell Minor. New York: Crowell.

———. 1989. *Heartland.* Illus. Wendell Minor. New York: Crowell.

Silverstein, Shel. 1974. *Where the sidewalk ends.* New York: HarperCollins.

———. 1981. *Light in the attic.* New York: Harper-Collins.

Smith, William Jay, and Carol Ra. 1992. *Behind the king's kitchen.* Illus. Jacques Hnizdovsky. Honesdale, PA: Wordsong/Boyds Mills Press.

Sneve, Virginia Driving Hawk, ed. 1989. *Dancing tepees: Poems of American Indian youth.* Illus. Stephen Gammell. New York: Holiday.

Soto, Gary. 1991. *A fire in my hands.* Illus. James M. Cardillo. New York: Scholastic.

———. 1992. *Neighborhood odes.* Illus. David Diaz. San Diego: Harcourt Brace.

Spier, Peter. 1961. *The fox went out on a chilly night.* New York: Doubleday.

———. 1986. *The star spangled banner.* Illus. Peter Spier. New York: Doubleday.

———. 1990. *Erie Canal.* New York: Doubleday.

Spilka, Arnold. 1994. *Monkeys write terrible letters.* Honesdale, PA: Wordsong/Boyds Mills Press.

Springer, Nancy. 1994. *Music of their hooves.* Illus. Sandy Rabinowitz. Honesdale, PA: Wordsong/Boyds Mills Press.

Stevenson, Robert Louis. 1905. *A child's garden of verses.* Illus. Jessie Willcox Smith. New York: Scribner.

Strickland, Michael. 1993. *Poems that sing to you.* Illus. Alan Leiner. Honesdale, PA: Wordsong/Boyds Mills Press.

Strickland, Dorothy, and Michael Strickland. 1994. *Families: Poems celebrating the African American Experience.* Illus. John Ward. Honesdale, PA: Wordsong/Boyds Mills Press.

Swenson, May. 1993. *The complete book of poems to solve.* New York: Macmillan.

Tejima, Keizaburo. 1987. *Owl lake.* New York: Philomel.

Terban, Marvin. 1994. *Time to rhyme: A rhyming dictionary.* Illus. Chris L. Demarest. Honesdale, PA: Wordsong/Boyds Mills Press.

Thayer, Ernest. 1988. *Casey at the bat.* Illus. Barry Moser. Boston: Godine.

Untermeyer, Louis. [1959] 1963. *The golden treasury of poetry.* Illus. Joan Walsh Anglund. New York: Golden Press.

Wadsworth, Olivia A., and Mary M. Rae. 1985. *Over in the meadow: A counting-out rhyme.* New York: Viking.

Wall, Steve, and Harvey Arden. 1990. *Wisdom-keepers: Meetings with Native American spiritual elders.* Hillsboro, OR: Beyond Words Publishers, Inc.

Watson, Clyde. 1978. *Catch me and kiss me and say it again.* Illus. Wendy Watson. New York: Philomel.

Westcott, Nadine B. 1980. *I know an old lady who swallowed a fly.* Illus. Nadine Westcott. Boston: Little, Brown.

Widerberg, Siv. 1974. *I'm like me.* New York: The Feminist Press.

Wildsmith, Brian. 1982. *Cat on the mat.* London: Oxford University Press.

Williams, Vera. 1983. *A chair for my mother.* New York: Greenwillow.

Worth, Valerie. [1976] 1986. *More small poems.* Illus. Natalie Babbitt. New York: Farrar, Straus & Giroux.

———. 1987a. *All the small poems.* Illus. Natalie Babbitt. New York: Farrar, Straus & Giroux.

———. 1987b. *Small poems.* Illus. Natalie Babbitt. New York: Farrar, Straus & Giroux.

———. 1995. "Crickets." In *A jar of tiny stars.* Ed. Bernice E. Cullinan. Honesdale, PA: Wordsong/Boyds Mills Press.

Yolen, Jane. 1987. *Owl moon.* Illus. John Schoenherr. New York: Putnam.

———. 1990. *Birdwatch: A book of poetry.* Illus. Ted Lewin. New York: Putnam.

———. 1992. *Street rhymes around the world.* Illus. 17 International Artists. Honesdale, PA: Wordsong/Boyds Mills Press.

———. 1993a. *Songs of summer.* Illus. Cyd Moore. Music. Adam Stemple. Honesdale, PA: Wordsong/Boyds Mills Press.

———. 1993b. *Weather report.* Illus. Annie Gusman. Honesdale, PA: Wordsong/Boyds Mills Press.

———. 1994a. *Jane Yolen's Old MacDonald songbook.* Musical arr. Adam Stemple. Illus. Rosekrans Hoffman. Honesdale, PA: Wordsong/Boyds Mills Press.

———. 1994b. *Sleep rhymes around the world.* Illus. 17 International Artists. Honesdale, PA: Wordsong/Boyds Mills Press.

———. 1995a. *Alphabestiary.* Illus. Allan Eitzen. Honesdale, PA: Wordsong/Boyds Mills Press.

———. 1995b. *Water Music.* Photos. Jason Stemple. Honesdale, PA: Wordsong/Boyds Mills Press.

Zim, Jacob, ed. 1975. *My shalom my peace: Paintings and poems by Arab and Israeli children.* Tel Aviv: Sabra Books.

Glossary

Alliteration the repetition of initial consonants (e.g., "big bad bear").

Anapest a metrical foot consisting of three syllables with two unaccented syllables followed by an accented one.

Anthology a collection of poems. A *specialized anthology* has works by several poets on one subject; a *generalized anthology* has works by many poets on many subjects; and an *individual anthology* contains the works of only one poet.

Anthropomorphism the giving of human qualities to animals or objects.

Apostrophe a figure of speech addressing things that cannot answer, a nonexistent person, or some abstract quality.

Approximation an attempt that is close to correct but not quite right.

Assonance similar vowel sounds in syllables that end with different consonant sounds (e.g., "galoshes make splishes and sploshes" [Bacmeister 1976]).

Ballad a form of verse to be sung, consisting of an exciting episode and told in narrative form.

Big Books oversize books used for group instruction.

Chapter book a book with chapters, episodic segments, and few illustrations.

Character map a visual display of relationships among characters.

Characterization the way in which an author makes a person or creature seem believable through words.

Cinquain a five-line stanza of varying meter and rhyme scheme; an unrhymed five-line stanza with two, four, six, eight, and two syllables.

Cliche an expression used so often it loses its freshness.

Community of learners people who help each other learn and share joy in seeing others learn.

Concrete poem a poem or verse written in a shape to extend the meaning of the words. It combines the graphic and visual aspects of writing to make a picture.

Connotation the emotional meaning of a word.

Conversations (Conversation poem) Discourse or conversation with an addressee and respondent. It may contain some element of satire.

Couplet two lines of verse with similar end rhymes. It can be considered a two-line stanza.

Cuing systems   cues that readers use to get meaning from print (e.g., graphophonic [the sounds the letters represent]; syntactic [the order of the words]; and semantic [the meaning of the words]).

Demonstrate   to show how by example.

Denotation   the dictionary definition of a word.

Diamante   a poem in the shape of a diamond. It begins with one word and grows word by word, line by line, then tapers off to one word at the bottom.

Didactic   preachy, moralistic.

Dramatic poetry   poems that incorporate dramatic techniques, such as dialogue, vigorous diction, tense situations, and emotional conflict.

Easy-to-read books   books with phrase-structured text, short lines, and a limited number of different vocabulary words.

Employ   to use something, to practice a new skill.

End papers   the insides of front and back covers of a book.

Expectation   the assumption that a child will learn readily.

Feedback   the return of information to a child; the response to comments or actions.

Free verse   poetry that uses irregular rhythmic cadence with variations in phrases, images, and syntactical patterns. Rhyme may or may not be present.

Genre   the classification of literature, literary forms, categories, and types.

Haiku   a form of Japanese poetry that states in three lines of five, seven, and five syllables a clear picture designed to arouse an emotion and suggest an insight.

Iamb (Iambus)   a metrical foot consisting of an unaccented syllable and an accented one. This is the most common metrical measure in English verse.

Imagery   words that appeal to the senses.

Immersion   the experience of being totally surrounded with something.

Integrated curriculum   school subjects combined in a comprehensive study organized across areas and unified through a common theme, thread, or topic.

Language style   the choice and arrangement of words.

Limerick   a form of light verse with a definite pattern: five anapestic lines of which the first, second, and fifth consist of three feet and rhyme, and the third and fourth consist of two feet and rhyme.

Line breaks   the places in a poem where the poet decides to end one line and begin another to accentuate the meaning of a poem.

List poem   a poem containing a list of things.

Literacy   the ability to read and write.

Literature-based curriculum   a school program in which many types of tradebooks are used in all areas. Students learn about and through literature.

Lyric   a brief poem marked by imagination, melody, and emotion creating a single unified impression.

Mask (Masque)   to pretend to be something else; in literature, to speak from another's voice.

Metaphor   an implied analogy or comparison, e.g., "A poem is a magical boat to ride/ in a sea of words with a rhyming tide." From "Poems" by Bobbi Katz, (Goldstein 1992).

Meter   the recurrence of a rhythmic pattern; the rhythm established by the regular occurrence of similar sound patterns.

Metrics the patterns or rhythm in poetry; the principles describing the nature of rhythms; prosody.

Model to show a good example of how to do something (e.g., reading poetry aloud).

Narrative poem a poem that tells a story; includes ballads and epics.

Onomatopoeia words that sound like their meaning.

Parody a work designed to ridicule another piece of work in a humorous fashion.

Pattern the repeated set of words or device.

Personification the giving of human traits to inanimate objects.

Picture book a book in which the illustrations extend the meaning of the words.

Poetic form the established rules for poems (e.g., sonnet, ballad, haiku, and limerick).

Poetic patterns the degree of regularity in rhythm, meter, and recurring accents at stated intervals (e.g., iambic pentameter, dactyllic dimeter, and rhythmic systems).

Point of view the perspective from which a writer or poet speaks: first person, third person, or omniscient narrator.

Predictable text rhythmic, melodic language; rhyming words; repeated words; repeated patterns.

Reading-writing workshop a regularly scheduled block of classroom time devoted to reading and writing.

Repetition the repeated use of words, sounds, or syntactic structures.

Rhyme words that sound alike (e.g., lake/make; run/fun).

Rhythm the recurring flow of strong (accented) and weak (unaccented) beats in language. The rhythmic unit within a line is called a foot: standard feet include iambic, trochaic, anapestic, dactyllic, spondaic, and pyrrhic.

Schema a reader's organized knowledge of the world. A network or category system that we develop as we receive new information.

Semantic mapping a visual way to organize information; a graphic organizer that shows relationships among facts, ideas, and categories. This method helps activate and build on a student's prior knowledge.

Sijo a type of Korean poetry, written in three lines with approximately forty-four syllables (because they are awkwardly long in English, they are presented in six lines instead of the traditional three). The first line usually states the theme, the second elaborates on it, and the third line is a twist on the theme or a resolution, sometimes called the antitheme.

Simile a stated comparison (e.g., "a baby's mouth is like a rose").

Student responsibility students take charge of what they learn and become responsible for seeking information and guidance.

Symbol an element with both figurative and literal meaning.

Tanka a type of Japanese poetry similar to haiku. It consists of thirty-one syllables arranged in five lines. The first and third lines consist of five syllables, the other lines are each of seven. Haiku seems to be the first three lines and the first seventeen syllables of tanka.

Theme the central or dominating idea; an abstract concept made vivid through character and image.

Time line a chronological series of dates used to mark significant events.

Trochee a metric foot consisting of an accented and an unaccented syllable, as in the word *hurry*.

Unity   the coordination of text and illustration.

Verisimilitude   an appearance of being true; a semblance of truth.

Verse   a unit of poetry, a metrical composition.

White space   the blank, empty space on a page. Poems generally have short lines that are set out on a page leaving a large amount of white space.

Word bank   a filing system for keeping track of new words for spelling or vocabulary, sometimes kept in a notebook or card file.

Writing workshop   a block of classroom time set aside for student writing. It includes holding mini-lessons and conferences, reading drafts, revising, and sharing and discussing writing.

Credits

Page 14: "Crickets" from *Small Poems* by Valerie Worth. Copyright © 1972 by Valerie Worth. Reprinted by permission of Farrar, Straus & Giroux.

Page 17: "Poems." Copyright © 1992 by Bobbi Katz. Reprinted by permission of the author.

Page 19: "My Name" from *Kim's Place* by Lee Bennett Hopkins. Copyright © 1974 by Lee Bennett Hopkins. Reprinted by permission of Curtis Brown, Ltd.

Page 19: "And Off He Went Just As Proud As You Please" from *You Know Who* by John Ciardi. Copyright © 1964 by John Ciardi. Copyright renewed in 1991 by Judith H. Ciardi. Reprinted by permission of Wordsong/Boyds Mills Press.

Page 23: "My Book" from *Somebody Catch My Homework* by David Harrison. Copyright © 1993 by David Harrison. Reprinted by permission of the author.

Page 25: "Things" from *Honey, I Love, and Other Love Poems* by Eloise Greenfield. Copyright © 1978 by Eloise Greenfield. Reprinted by permission of HarperCollins.

Page 39: "Talkaty Talker" from *Talkaty Talker* by Molly Manley. Copyright © 1994 Molly Hollingsworth Manley. Reprinted by permission of Boyds Mills Press.

Pages 42–43: *The Black Pearl* by Scott O'Dell. Copyright © 1967 by Scott O'Dell. Reprinted by permission of Houghton Mifflin Co. All rights reserved.

Page 47: "Lobster" from *What If?: Just Wondering Poems* by Joy N. Hulme. Copyright © 1993 by Joy N. Hulme. Reprinted by permission of Wordsong/Boyds Mills Press.

Page 48: "First Steps" by Brod Bagert. Copyright © 1993 by Brod Bagert. Reprinted by permission of the author.

Page 49: "Will We Ever See" from *Creatures of Earth, Sea, and Sky* by Georgia Heard. Copyright © 1992 by Georgia Heard. Reprinted by permission of Wordsong/Boyds Mills Press.

Page 74: "A Writing Kind of Day" from *Water Planet* by Ralph Fletcher. Copyright © 1991 by Ralph Fletcher. Reprinted by permission of Marian Reiner.

Page 74: "Hummingbird" from *Creatures of Earth, Sea, and Sky* by Georgia Heard. Copyright © 1992 by Georgia Heard. Reprinted by permission of Wordsong/Boyds Mills Press.